Yes Is Better Than No

by

**BYRD
BAYLOR**

ILLUSTRATIONS BY LEONARD CHANA

YES IS BETTER THAN NO
by Byrd Baylor

Illustrations by
Leonard Chana

Text Design by
Pegasus Promotions

Copyright © 1991, 1990, 1977, 1973, 1972 by Byrd Baylor

Library of Congress Cataloging in Publication Data

Baylor, Byrd
    Yes is better than no.

SUMMARY: Focuses on the problems and experiences of a small group of Papago
Indians who have left the reservation to live in a ghetto in Tucson, Arizona.
    [1. Papago Indians — Fiction. 2. Indians of North America — Fiction] I. Title.

PZ7.B3435Ye   [Fic]   76-57705

ISBN 0-918080-53-3 (paper)
ISBN 0-918080-59-2 (cloth)

Chapter 1 of this book originally appeared as "Yes is Better than No" in the September
1972 issue of McCall's Magazine. Chapter 3 originally appeared as "The Winner" in the
March 1972 issue of Redbook. Chapter 4 originally appeared as "A Faint Glow Under
the Ashes" in the July 1973 issue of Redbook.

Yes

Is Better

Than

No

TREASURE CHEST PUBLICATIONS, INC.
1802 W. GRANT RD., SUITE #101 (85745)
P.O. BOX 5250
TUCSON, AZ 85703-0250

Maria Vasquez

Down the street from the B-29 bar is the shrine of St. Jude. Stiff armed and staring into space, St. Jude. Dry bougainvillea leaves in his plaster hair today, but fewer candles than usual. Yesterday a drunk vomited on him, poor man, pouring out his excuses, his grief, his thirty-nine-cent Thunderbird wine. They had to take away the candles.

Today Maria passes by on her way to the B-29 bar but she only glances. Not so much as the sign of the cross. Not really even a nod.

Jude, I'll be back. Don't worry. Maybe I'll spend the night. We'll watch the moon rise together yet.

How would it be to spend the night with a saint anyway?

Her mother had once said, "Remember, nothing is impossible to this saint. For myself, I ask St. Martin first, but then second I go to St. Jude for impossible needs . . . for impossible situations. Situations like this life." And she had smiled as she said it.

That was before Maria left the reservation. So long ago that nothing had ever been impossible enough to force her to seek out St. Jude. And now, dear God, she knows him well enough to dispense with formality. Just half a nod. . . .

Maria walks down the dusty sidewalk slowly, slowly, evenly as Indian women walk. Though she is still young, her hips don't swing; she doesn't dance along the way Mexican girls do. Instead, she moves her feet on the city sidewalk as though she were moving barefoot across the desert. As though that journey might take all night, all week, a lifetime. The foot falls solidly to meet the earth, feels the pull of the earth. A heavy walk, but easy and animal-like. No man who watches women walk here mistakes the black-eyed, black-haired Indian girls for Mexicans. You can tell that walk a block away.

She comes to the B-29 bar. Going into its darkness means passing from the harsh reality of the town into the safety of a mystical home. A sacrament, crossing that doorway. Believe me, Jude, there are more sacraments than those the priest mentions.

Outside, the light of the hot desert sun; inside, the dimness of a cave. Well, ceremonial wine houses on the reservation are dim too.

Outside, Tucson street noises; inside, the easy sounds of Papago language. Papago and Spanish too, not much English. And the English that is spoken by Indians sounds like Indian, anyway, resting in the hollows of the throat, each word coming out soft as a baby rabbit.

Papago language has the right sound for people of the desert. It holds the quiet of the mesas; it rolls words into the natural shapes of breathing so they come from the mouth still soft around the edges, small winds that might blow across a hill of summer weeds. That kind of sound.

Papago is a language much too quiet for anger. Let them have English for anger and authority and commands and papers to sign. Even a social worker would not sound so important, perhaps, if she made Papago sounds instead of words that come flying out of the mouth stiff as boards. You feel their sharp splinters in the air . . . .

Maria slides across the beer-sticky wooden bench and sinks back against the crumbling pink plaster which clings to the adobe walls. Breathes in . . . breathes out . . . believes it is the only breath she has drawn all day.

The mood here is slow and quiet in spite of the deafening jukebox music. Purifying in its terrible intensity. Time never moves here. Noon, midnight, three a.m.; it's all the same at the B-29.

Maria's friend, Rose, comes to sit beside her, just sits, doesn't ask anything.

Maria unties a handkerchief, puts fifteen cents on the wooden table. Rose adds thirty-five cents more.

The bartender, Anglo, burly, with levis and boots and red cowboy shirt beneath his dirty white apron, comes over and puts down a pitcher of beer and four glasses. There will be others at the table later.

It isn't for a long time yet, maybe half an hour, that Maria says, "I don't have the house anymore."

"You didn't pay?"

"I paid. I'm paid for another week still."

She finishes a glass of beer, pours another and sits looking into its depth. "The man that brought all the papers—he came and nailed it up today because it's not fit to live in. That one."

Rose shrugs.

They both accept the fact that the invisible rules by which their lives are governed are completely, desperately, insanely senseless. There is no use trying to understand them. Haven't they all been told a thousand times: "But those are our regulations, Mrs. Garcia. There is nothing we can do about it . . . ." "Sorry, Mr. Escalante, but we all have to abide by certain rules . . . ." "No, Mrs. Gonzales, if we let *you,* they'd all be asking . . . ."

So Maria had not said to the man from the health department that, yes, she knew it was bad with all those holes in the walls but still it was all she could afford and where would she and the five children sleep tonight if he went ahead and nailed that board across the door?

Now she only says to Rose, "Since I'm paid up for almost a week, we'll sleep in the yard. Maybe it won't rain."

"Maybe."

"At least he didn't say the yard wasn't fit to live in. Just the house."

"You sure?"

She isn't sure, of course.

On the reservation you know certain rules that haven't changed since the people came up from the underworld. But here in town they change the rules every day. Out there when the fine balance of the world is upset there are still things that can be done. But there's no ceremony or song or blessing or magic in a medicine man's bag that will help you against the white people who come to nail boards across your door.

Your stomach twists and doubles and knots when you talk to those people — the ones who make rules which no one could ever guess beforehand. It takes darkness and Indian voices and sometimes a pitcher of beer to let your insides settle again. It takes music and a man to come over and sit close enough so you can feel his leg against you and see the dark hairs on his wrists and breathe the man smell of him. Sometimes it takes the closeness of a man in bed all night and even then, God knows, you can still wake up afraid.

"Lucky it's so hot now," Rose says. "Everybody sleeps out anyway."

"Sure."

The bar is filling, and through the open door you can see that the sky is purple against the mountains, almost dark. It is a good time of day. All those who have been working at the rich houses on the east side of town are home again, the men who have been doing yard work, the women who have been doing housework. There are more women than men, of course, because it is easier to find housework than yard work.

The bus stops at the corner and through the open door you can see them getting off, going home. They're slow, tired. A few come into the B-29, pushing back their wide-brimmed straw hats, peering into the dimness.

One of the men is Lopez. Rose has been waiting for him, so she moves across the table from Maria and Lopez slides into the booth and puts his arm around Rose, touching her breasts. He speaks to her first in Papago even though it is only a greeting. Hi. They pour another glass of beer.

Lopez has been working. Now he brings out five dollars and says, "Okay, you can buy his goddamn fly tonight."

Rose holds tightly to her glass and nods.

Lopez waves across the room to an old man, a Mexican, wearing somebody's give-away white tennis shoes with his levis and work shirt. No laces. The shoes would fall off if he picked his feet up from the floor, but he glides carefully along.

"You got the money tonight? You want the cure?

Lopez holds up the five dollars.

Rose says, "I want the cure."

"All right then," the old man says. "I got the fly."

He takes a small package from his levi pocket – a fly in a small wax paper bag. Shakes it.

"Wait a minute now," Lopez says. "If it doesn't work do you give us back our money?"

The old man looks at him sideways, offended. "It works, man."

Maria is only glad that no one is trying to cure her of the pleasure of a glass of beer. But Rose ... she goes to jail so often for it.

"We should start with a full pitcher," the old man says, standing over them. A medicine man almost.

"Then you buy," Lopez says. "You got the money now."

But as they motion to the bartender, they notice that someone who doesn't belong there is standing in the doorway. The regulars always feel uneasy when a white stranger comes to the door and looks them over. This place should be a sanctuary from Anglos. Of course, you expect the

6

police now and then; you just try not to look up at them even though you feel your hands tighten, your stomach flip.

This man is young and wears levis and a blue work shirt and a fine big Navajo silver and turquoise belt buckle. He looks all right, maybe even friendly, but everyone sees immediately that he is carrying a clipboard and papers. That's bad . . . .

He stands at the door looking around the dim room and then strides in long certain steps over to the bartender and holds out his hand.

"Henry Cunningham." He smiles seriously.

The bartender puts down a bottle of tequila and slowly extends his hand.

"Listen," the young man says, "maybe you'd do me a little favor." You can tell he is used to favors. "We're doing a study at the university on motivational backgrounds among off-reservation Indians, and . . . ."

Motor vehicle something or other is what it sounds like to those close enough to hear. The bartender wipes his hands and squints. He's still waiting to hear what the favor is. So is everybody else. The young man goes on talking about how he tried to set up a meeting for this afternoon over at the Southside Hall—notices on the bulletin board, letters to the Indian Center, everything— "But no one showed up to be interviewed."

"Yeah," says the bartender.

"And before that, home interviews. But of course nobody ever came to the door. You know how it is."

"Yeah," says the bartender.

"And there's a deadline for this study. So I was wondering . . . could I ask some of your customers a question or two?"

Maria turns her face toward the peeling plaster, doesn't look back. But she can hear the bartender say, "Aw, you won't do no good here."

At least he is that loyal to his customers. He *tries*, but the man with the papers in his hand says, "Listen, it's painless. Anyway, I only need to talk to the Indians."

Not an Indian looks up now, though the Mexicans relax and watch the young man pay for his beer and select a ballpoint pen from among the three in his shirt pocket.

Maria's table is near the back of the room. She can hear his voice at the next booth even though she tries not to.

The thing is that you don't know which Anglos are the ones you *have* to answer. You don't know which ones can really board up a house or take away a welfare check or even put you in jail or take your children to foster homes. You don't know which are the papers you *have* to sign. Almost all white people speak in a way that sounds so important, how can you tell?

For instance, there was that social worker who had told Maria not to have any more babies. So when the last one was born what could she do but hide her when anyone from welfare came around. Hide her or say, "Look, I'm keeping my cousin's baby." Even now Maria isn't certain whether that woman could come and take Carmen away.

Now the young man with the papers is standing at their table. The two women look down but Lopez and the old man standing over the pitcher say hello.

"You people *are* Indian, aren't you? Papago?"

They nod.

"Mind if I sit down a minute?"

Maria moves closer to the wall and he sits beside her, puts his glass of beer on the table. The jukebox is quiet for a moment and the fly moves helplessly within its wax paper bag in the center of the table.

The young man starts to say something, notices the fly, and stops. No one answers his questioning look, however, and he turns back to the clipboard.

"Now then, just let me chat with you a few minutes. This won't take long." He offers a pack of cigarettes and they all smoke silently, waiting.

The paper on top of the clipboard is titled *Motivational Background and Current Achievement Levels Among Off-Reservation Papago Indians.*

"We just want to find out whether you were encouraged as youngsters to prepare yourselves for good jobs. Encouraged or discouraged . . . ."

Lopez moves his hands from Rose's unbuttoned shirt front to some less noticeable spot under the table. The old man remains standing, watching the occasional movements of the captured fly.

"Let's put it this way: Have you achieved your own personal employment goals? Were you able to become whatever it was you dreamed of being, and if not—"

They look at his face to see whether an answer is expected.

The music starts again, this time a wildly plaintive song in Spanish. Lost love and tears. The fly which had been quiet for a long time now begins to move, frantically dancing. Maria, Rose and Lopez all notice this and laugh gently.

The young man laughs too. "I agree with you. They're crazy sounding questions, all right. Every one of them."

The three want to laugh again because he has misunderstood but they stop themselves and look back at him, stiff, polite and serious.

"Who was the most important motivating figure for you between the ages of six to twelve, twelve to fourteen, fourteen to eighteen. That is . . . who made you *want* to succeed?"

They give this some thought.

"Your parents? Tribal leaders? Classmates? Anybody who encouraged you to go ahead and make it in the world. Anybody who gave you confidence in yourself."

They look at each other.

"That could be your teachers, of course."

Yes, they all agree. Certainly. Teachers.

"Do you believe there is any correlation between your earning power today and your educational opportunities?"

"By all means," Lopez answers for them.

The three Indians at the table, like all the others in the B-29 this evening, have been interviewed by similar young Anglos on similar topics. They have each learned long ago to try to give answers which will most please the questioner. At times this is hard to figure out, but they try. Everyone knows, for instance, that white people are very pleased when Indian girls say they wish to become nurses or teachers. So most of them give those answers.

Another thing. If a yes or no answer is required, they try to say yes. In most of their dealings with white people Indians find that it is easier and more polite to say yes than no. This saves arguing and has, of course, nothing at all to do with one's actions. It simply puts off any ill feeling, makes the moment happier.

Maria speaks so softly that the young man has to lean forward to hear her answers. He has jotted down the facts so far: Papago. Age 29. Five children. Husband's occupation: laborer (unemployed). Husband's boyhood ambition: priest.

Maria had been undecided whether to say priest or doctor since white people like both answers. But thinking how long it had been since she had seen Joe Vasquez and how funny he would look out there in the Yuma melon fields dressed in a priest's robes, she made her choice. "Yes, he always wished to be a priest."

Wife's occupation: housework. Girlhood ambition: nurse.

"And your children. Have they expressed vocational preferences yet? Told you what they wish to become?"

"Nurses."

"All of them?"

"All the girls. Yes."

"And their ages?"

She pauses, can't remember, guesses. "Two . . . five . . . seven, no, eight . . . nine. The girls."

"And even those very young ones have expressed an opinion?"

"Oh, yes. They all want to be nurses. And the boy, a doctor."

"A doctor. He's certain of that?"

She nods. "If not that, then a priest."

There is a pause but the young man finally fills in his questionnaire. His eyes keep returning to the fly.

He has to ask. "Whose . . . fly?"

The old man says, "It's mine. But it's for her." He nods his head toward Rose.

"It's to put in my beer," she says. "It's a cure. You know."

"Oh, yes. In your beer."

The old man pours four glasses of beer—for himself, Maria, Rose and Lopez. "You want some more?" he asks the young man with the clipboard.

"Oh, no thanks. No." He gathers up his papers and stands watching the old man shake the fly from the bag into his hand and close his stiff fingers over it. From time to time he shakes his hand and holds it up to his ear like a great earth-brown seashell.

"Now, you can just tell me to mind my own business if you like . . . but did I understand that this lady is going to put the fly in her beer?"

"No," the fly's owner explains patiently. "No, I have to put it in when she's not looking. Otherwise no cure."

"And if you don't mind my asking, what is it that a fly in beer cures?"

They all look at him, but they wait for the old man to answer. After all, it's his fly.

At last the old man tells him. "It cures beer drinking."

And the young man goes away.

As soon as he is out of sight, the B-29 relaxes again. There is a different sound to the arguments, to the laughter, to the singing, to the curses, even a different shape to people's motions. Time stretches out again, flat as it should be on a hot summer night.

People come and go at the booth where Maria sits but she does not tell anyone else about the house being boarded up. She doesn't want to think of it herself either. After all, that's the reason she is here, to put it off for a moment more. She laughs now and then, taps her foot to the music, wishes the B-29 were a place for dancing. It would be good to dance all night. When you're dancing it doesn't really matter whether there is a board nailed across the front door or not.

A tug at her arm. "Mama. Hey, mama." It is one of her girls, Anna, the oldest, ten. She is holding the baby heavily on her hip, her bare feet sidestepping the cigarette butts glowing on the cement floor.

"They're fussing because they can't get in the house. They want somebody to take the board off the door."

Maria takes the baby and gets up. Rose reaches for the baby, cuddles her a minute, hands her back to Anna.

"Okay, we'll go." One last sip of beer and they leave, Maria carrying the baby now, rocking her as she moves. One last glance back at Rose, at the old man whose left hand is still cupped around the fly.

It's dark and they walk home slowly. Past the Chinese grocery store, past the Friendship Rescue Mission, past the shrine of St. Jude (tomorrow, Jude) and around the corner to the dusty alley where they stop in front of the boarded-up shack with the **CONDEMNED** sign in the center of the front door. Under it, the picture of the Virgin of Guadalupe and the notice: *Welcome to this house where our Lady of Guadalupe is Queen. This is a Catholic house. Propaganda of* *other religions will not be admitted.* It is written in both Spanish and English.

"We could get in," Anna says, "with a rock or with a knife. Either one."

"We better not. It's against the law."

There are three mattresses, all thin, on the ground. One is a double-bed size and the other two are singles. There are several cardboard boxes, some of them for dirty clothes and some for clean, one for pots and pans and dishes.

The girls have already organized things. Anna has a single mattress to herself. Amelia and Jane, both tiny, share the other single. The baby, Carmen, and the boy, Errol Flynn, will sleep with Maria. Some of them are almost asleep now, their heads on the mattresses, their feet and legs dangling in the dirt. Maria looks in the boxes, finds sheets and scraps of blankets to put over them.

"Didn't you leave me a tortilla?"

"Beans too, a little."

The wood stove is under a mesquite tree. Maria finds a cold tortilla in the pan and folds it around a small mound of frijoles and a piece of green chile. Then she walks back across the yard and sits down on the bed, takes off her shoes, moves her toes in the dirt.

While she is eating, the girls sit up and begin to ask her, "Did you dance, Mama? Did you drink beer?"

"Go to sleep."

"Did you have to pay, Mama? A man bought you beer, no?"

She can barely see their faces around her. "Go to sleep." And then she says it in Papago too.

But no one sleeps yet. Finally Maria says into the darkness, "Who wants to be a nurse? Anna, you want to be a nurse someday?"

"Not me."

"Amelia? A nurse?"

"I hate nurses. Nobody's going to make me be a nurse."

13

"I hate nurses too," says Jane.

Maria smiles to herself. "Okay," she says. "Sleep."

There is Mexican music from somebody's radio. A car that won't start tries and dies again and again. The stars are very bright now, clear wide patterns to follow across the sky. Maria knows only a few of the Papago names for stars, none in English. She lies looking up, searching for the five stars which mark the touch of *I'itoi's* fingers, for once during the creation of the world the sky began to fall and *I'itoi* thrust up his great arm to hold the sky in place . . . .

Carmen sleeps next to Maria. On the other side, Errol Flynn, the only boy. He is looking up too.

"Errol Flynn, a doctor? You want to be a doctor?"

"Not me," he says, sleepy.

They are all quiet now, only a stray puppy wandering from bed to bed, sniffing each child. And that car still trying to start.

Even though the bed is so crowded that Maria is lying on the edge with her hand resting in the warm sand, she feels that she is sleeping alone. In any bed without a man, you lie alone.

Every night Maria goes to sleep thinking of a man unless she is too tired to think at all. Different men for different reasons. Sad reasons that lead you down the street to St. Jude. But others too—reasons that keep you wanting to live.

She thinks most often of her husband, Joe Vasquez. Jose. It's true she may forget him all day when things are bad, but this time of night she remembers how he used to lie in the darkness and tell her stories of movies. Any movie. One he had seen that day or the day before or one from years ago.

Everybody used to know Joe Vasquez as the man who liked movies. It was true. His hunger for movies was almost as great as his thirst for wine, and if he had those two pleasures there was nothing else that really mattered to him—maybe two pints of wine a day and a movie once or twice a week. If he'd been rich, then a movie every day.

So whenever they could find the money Joe used to spend the afternoon at the cheapest theater in town. He always walked to the bus with Maria when she went to do housework, and he would stay watching the story over and over until time to go to the bus to meet her in the evening. They would walk home together then but he never told her the story until they were in bed.

Poor Joe Vasquez, sick from years of too little food and too much wine. Pains in his stomach. The Anglo doctor at the clinic had said it was from his own drinking, but the *maka:ii* had found that it was rattlesnake sickness and, another time, whirlwind sickness, and Joe seemed better for a while. But he couldn't work a full day anymore. Sometimes two or three hours, but he would be shaking at the end of that time.

Whenever he was in jail, of course he had to stay the full ten days. Maria never had enough money to bail him out, but she would save what she could so that there would be a bottle of tokay waiting for him and movie money hidden behind the picture of St. Francis Xavier.

It was nice, hearing those stories. Joe always told them slowly as though he were one of the old Papago storytellers measuring out his stories through the winter nights.

How many nights—surely a hundred—had Joe described the strange green jungle where Tarzan and Jane escaped from tigers and lions and gorillas. Maria had never seen it herself but she almost knew the sound of the bird cries there and the way the water closed over the round eyes of hidden hungry crocodiles. That was the land Joe liked most of all, and theirs was the way of living he most admired. Free and wild as animals. They often talked of how much easier it was for Tarzan and Jane to survive than for their own ancestors, those Indians who had gone as bare but who had toiled so hard to stay alive, had walked such rocky land, had eaten roots and mesquite beans and cactus fruit while Tarzan only reached overhead for a banana.

"What language did they speak?" she once asked him, filled with wonder.

"Mostly sign language," he said. "But a little English too. Not good English though. Not school English."

And Maria had felt she knew those two. It was in honor of that beautiful dark-haired Jane who could swing so gracefully from the branch of a jungle tree that they had called their own child Jane. Actually, Jane Ann because you need one saint's name too, of course.

And the boy, Errol Flynn. He too was named for someone Maria had never seen, but Joe had described his wavy hair, his small mustache, his marvelous flashing sword, the way he leapt over chairs and tables and fought up and down long flights of stairs in dark ugly castles.

By now Maria has forgotten the names of the countries but she remembers that this man laughed aloud as he fought. Joe often said he was the bravest of all men in the movies. In battles he was the one to volunteer for the dangerous ride over the white hills by moonlight. He was the one to fight on alone while the others made it safely over the drawbridge. He was the one who carried the wounded to safety before they found that he too had been shot . . . .

Maria thinks of that Errol Flynn now as she sees that her own small son Errol Flynn has rolled off the mattress and is lying on his back in the dirt, asleep, his thumb in his mouth.

Tarzan and Jane were without a house too. At least Joe never spoke of one. They probably lay down on a mat woven of soft green grasses, not a smelly mattress from the Salvation Army store. They probably had a pillow stuffed with flower petals.

And then Jane had a man, a strong naked man with a leopard skin wrapped around him. But Maria sleeps alone in the back yard. Well, after all, this is no movie.

CHAPTER 2

St. Jude

You don't need to be a Catholic to know this saint.

An old Papago woman has just stopped to light a candle. She stands there, her scarf drawn tight around her head, holding in her hand a cut-off notice from the electric company. She moves slowly, stands with dignity. After all, her knees won't bend anymore even to a saint. She holds the paper toward him, shrugs ever so slightly, and passes on down the sidewalk.

Next a young girl, already feeling heavy in the belly but still trying to hide it. She looks down the street before she brings out a small photograph of her boyfriend and attaches it with a paper clip to a row of pictures hanging from a wire above the saint's head, mostly dark unsmiling boys in uniform. Army privates. One or two sailors, too. The girl touches the photograph with her fingers, then turns and runs. Her problem may be a woman's problem, but she still runs like a child.

You don't have to *say* anything here. Like a Papago medicine man, St. Jude knows instantly what the trouble is. Maybe he can't help you, but he knows just the same. No need to explain everything in words the way Anglos do.

This is a neighborhood shrine. It exists because someone's prayers to Jude were answered once. You know that someone must have said, "Help me out now, Jude, and I'll build you a good shrine there by the patio gate. A fifty dollar statue. A grotto made of the biggest rocks we can find. An electric light bulb to hang at the entrance. Better yet, Christmas tree lights twisting in and out among plastic flowers. And each year on your feast day something new — plaster cherubs, cement floor. Something."

Besides the pictures of boys in uniform there are wedding pictures, school pictures, a jockey standing beside a horse, a plump smiling couple embracing. And dozens of hospital identification bracelets, those little plastic-covered bends which fit around the wrist. Tiny tin amulets, too, in the shape of hearts, legs, hands, feet — wherever the pain is centered. And for all-over pain, the pain of a woman whose man is gone, the flame of a candle glowing all night through red glass.

There are house keys hanging in clusters from the curved ceiling. Car keys too. Part of a bridal bouquet. A dime-store ring with a lavender stone. A cross woven of bear grass, yucca, and devil's claw to hang around the saint's neck. Paper flowers, orange and pink and blue, in coffee cans and vases. Plastic lilies, faded now by summer rains, grouped around the strongbox which is locked and cemented into the floor at the saint's feet, a slit in the top for donations.

Once in a while someone leaves a seashell or a peacock feather to make the shrine more beautiful, for these are Indians who still remember shrines out on the reservation, not shrines to saints at all, but special places where the spirits are willing to accept small tokens from the living. Objects from earth or sky or sea . . . as well as something pretty from the dime store.

At night with the glow of many candles and the Christmas tree lights and the arms of the chinaberry tree moving above the grotto and the cane and oleander whispering by the fence, the shrine of St. Jude becomes magically beautiful. A place where miracles could happen. You forget the street noises and the hot rods and police sirens and broken wine bottles along the curb.

By day St. Jude himself seems smaller and the dust shows on the plastic flowers and the bright sunlight diminishes the glow of the candles. It is always best to visit the shrine at night.

St. Jude, saint of the impossible. We come to you only as a last resort, good friend.

Of course there are plenty of other saints in the churches, the large old St. Francis at the mission, the powerful St. Francis you make a pilgrimage all the way to Magdalena to see, other neighborhood saints too. Then the small shrines that people have in the corners of their houses, sometimes no more than a votive light and a photograph.

But St. Jude is a good saint for the Papago people because they too accept the impossible. Accept without question. The people of St. Jude aren't those who make choices, who say I won't take this kind of life, I demand something different. St. Jude's people are the ones who say, "So this is the way it is then. And if there is any change, you can thank good luck or bad luck for it. And you're a fool if you don't take whatever happiness comes along and take it quickly and take it without asking questions . . . because it may not come again."

St. Jude does not withhold his assistance from whores or drunks or thieves. He knows what is possible and what is not, that's all. And his people don't expect too much from him either.

CHAPTER 3

MRS. DOMINGO

Mrs. Domingo is pretending she can't speak English. She is seated on a low stool, her head bent over the basket she is weaving.

"Look here at this old squaw, hon. She don't speak a word of English."

"Well, I wish she'd say something in Indian then. How can we get her to say something?"

The man with the camera stands in front of Mrs. Domingo, raises his right hand, says 'HOW' and howls with laughter, bending over nearly double.

Mrs. Domingo does not even glance up.

"I'd like to get a picture of Sandra sitting up there on the Indian's lap or something," the woman says.

"Well, hell," the man says. "You gonna try saying that in sign language?" But then he goes up to the edge of the platform and tries to catch Mrs. Domingo's eye. "We take-um picture of you and the kid. See?"

Now Sandra backs off. "I'm not gonna sit on the Indian's lap. I don't care."

"She won't hurt you."

"I don't care."

They stand there for a while longer, but Mrs. Domingo does not seem to be aware of them. Not until they have moved on to the copper mining display does she shift her position on the stool and reach for the bottle of strawberry pop on the floor beside her.

She does not need to watch her work this closely. If a group of Papago women were sitting together under a ramada making baskets it would be a time for chatting and laughter and long comfortable silences. But here behind a roped off display of baskets and pottery she is not at ease.

Every year Mrs. Domingo and Mrs. Reyes show Papago baskets and give weaving demonstrations at the county fair. They sit on a little platform under a rope sign which says **LOCAL PAPAGO INDIAN CRAFTS**, and they hand out mimeographed sheets of information on the Papago tribe.

Sometimes they talk to the people who stand watching them. They don't mind telling them how they cut yucca or how far they walk for bear grass or how to distinguish a fine basket from a poorly made one. They don't mind people asking how old they are. They don't even mind when people ask if they live in tepees.

But then somebody has to ask them just exactly how many hours it takes to make a basket. The two old women always look at each other, each one hoping the other will make a guess at it. Their looks say, Who would know that? Who just sits down to make a basket and doesn't get up to pat tortillas or stir the beans or do some washing or go to the store? Maybe a week goes by. Maybe a month. Maybe the summer . . . a long time, that's all, a long time.

While they are deciding what to answer, somebody is sure to say, whispering, "Time means nothing to these people, you know."

And it is just about then that Mrs. Domingo decides not to speak English for awhile. Sometimes they take turns.

And sometimes they have their own joke. How long does it take to make a basket? Mrs. Domingo will look out over her gold-rimmed glasses and ask quietly, "White man's time or Indian time?"

Anglos usually think this over and say, "Well, white man's time, I guess. Regular time."

"But how would I know that? I'm an Indian." No smiling, of course. Not the slightest hint of amusement in her voice.

Then the two old ladies in their long flowered cotton dresses and white stockings can go back to their baskets and their strawberry pop for a while because the conversation is usually over. They can think about it, that comfortable feeling that comes from recognizing Indian time . . . each day unmarked by the hands of a clock unless you go to work for a white lady. She'll prize punctuality above all else. Foolish of her, though . . . .

This morning Mrs. Reyes has been down at the other end of the building watching the final judging of decorated cakes. This is what she likes best of all the entries — high, many-tiered white cakes with swirls of pink and white flowers on pale green stems. Now she comes back and climbs stiffly up on the platform and Mrs. Domingo gets up to take her turn at walking around.

First she pauses by the jars of clear amber pickled peaches and cactus jelly and fig preserves. Then she stops to admire a heavily starched blue and white crocheted cup and saucer, goes on to squash and corn and pumpkins. These she touches one by one, remembering the corn and melon patches her father had planted on the reservation . . . thin green shoots coming up from the hard desert earth, always at the mouth of a wash where they could catch the sudden torrents of water from the summer storms.

Yes, her father used to speak to the corn as he planted it, encouraging it to grow. He spoke separately to the squash, to the beans, to the melons. She would like for her grand-children to know some of those old planting songs now, perhaps some of the harvest songs, but the words are hazy in her mind. Not for fifty years has she heard somebody sing:

Blue evening falls,
Blue evening falls.
All around me
Corn tassels are trembling.

Well, you can't stand there all day fingering the corn tassels, admiring the colors of the squash. Mrs. Domingo moves on.

One thing she likes about the fair is that she goes home each day with a sack full of free samples, prizes, gifts of unbelievable variety . . . goes home and spreads them out on the oilcloth of the kitchen table for everyone to share.

Slivers of cheese in wax paper. Pamphlets on civil defense, guest ranches, waterless cooking, and copper mining. Calendars. Pencils. Matches. Balloons. A pen with a purple plastic flower glowing from the end of it. A tape measure. Coupons for free dancing lessons. A tiny American flag on a pin. Nutrition chart and calorie counter (neither tamales nor tortillas nor frijoles are listed). Bottle openers. Ruler made of venetian blind slat. Plastic fly swatter. Thread in a folder. Buttons which say *AVIS* and *HERTZ* and *I'M PROUD TO BE AN AMERICAN*.

Now Mrs. Domingo writes her name and address, very slowly, very carefully, on an entry blank for a free sewing machine. Another for a color television, already on display and showing a group of men sitting at a table talking. They have blue faces and grey hands which they move angrily as they speak.

Mrs. Domingo realizes that both the sewing machine and the television require electricity, and of course there are many times when the electricity in her house is turned off. Only last night she had taken a pink cut-off notice over to St. Jude just in case he could find a way to help her out. Not that she minds cooking outside, but in town wood is expensive . . . fifty cents a bundle. It would be fine if Jude could help her come across some good mesquite somewhere.

On her way back to her basket making, she stops at the Kon Tiki swimming pool display, a life-size color photograph of a swimming pool and, grouped around it, at least a dozen beautiful suntanned models in two-piece swimming suits. The girls sit on green plastic grass. Mrs. Domingo looks sideways at them, notes their nakedness, their long thin bodies so different from the shape of Papago nakedness.

"Come on, Grandma. You want to win yourself a big Kon Tiki pool?"

Mrs. Domingo looks around, realizes he is talking to her. "Sure. Sure." She reaches for one of the papers and writes her name. Elma Domingo. She takes a certain pride in knowing how to fill up these papers now that she's done it so many times, though for the first two years at the fair she had been too shy to put her name on anything.

Now she pushes the folded paper through the slot in the box and goes back and tells Mrs. Reyes, "A pool, a television, a sewing machine. You should sign up too."

But Mrs. Reyes has only been coming to the fair for two years. She isn't ready for that. "I don't like to put my name on their papers. You don't know what you might be signing."

This is the first day of the fair and Mrs. Domingo is too tired to stop by St. Jude's on the way home. But on the second day she stops and looks in her brown paper sack for some little gift, finally selects the tiny American flag and pins it to the woven cross which hangs from the saint's neck. She also puts a dime in the strongbox and lights a candle, doesn't say anything at all.

Then, on the third day of the fair Mrs. Domingo wins that Kon Tiki pool.

There must be two or three thousand people gathered around the stage when a girl in a fringed leather skirt and sequined cowboy shirt draws the name and hands it to a man who calls out over the microphone, "Mrs. Domingo. Elma Domingo, you lucky lady, wherever you are . . . ."

Casual as though she were stopping by to pick up a box of surplus commodities over at welfare, she says, "Oh yes, that's my name. That's me."

It takes a few minutes for her to get down from her platform. She walks slowly, still clutching a large flat basket in her hands. Mrs. Reyes and all the people from the nearby booths go with her. When she hesitates they push her forward.

There is a stir when the crowd finally parts to let the old Papago woman move up the steps to the stage. Laughter and cheers and two or three flashbulbs. The girls in swimming suits gather around and Mrs. Domingo stands looking down at the floor. The man who, according to the announcement, is international president of Kon Tiki pools, gives her his card and a large envelope of papers and tells her his personal representative will call on her Monday.

He looks disturbed when he reads her address and there is some whispering between the men in business suits, but the international president pats her on the back again anyway. Somebody turns on a tape recorder. "Mrs. Domingo, this is a lifelong dream for you, I imagine . . . owning your own Kon Tiki pool?"

Mrs. Domingo shakes her head. "No, no. I never thought of it before I put my name on the paper."

"Well, I'm sure that now your life will — uh. I'm sure that you will enjoy the gracious living that comes with a fine swimming pool."

But Mrs. Domingo looks carefully at the basket in her hands, runs her fingers around the edge of it, appears to be studying it for defects.

"Now tell the people, Mrs. Domingo, have you ever been swimming?"

"Not in a swimming pool, no." Mrs. Domingo begins to climb back down the three steps from the stage to the floor. She's too old for all this climbing up and down. She nods to them, takes the rest of the papers they thrust at her and returns to her basket display.

When they have sat there quietly for a while, Mrs. Reyes murmurs, "Maybe you could ask for the sewing machine instead."

Mrs. Domingo shrugs, turns up her hands. Then she smiles for the first time. Smiles as though she is beginning to understand a strange and marvelous puzzle. That St. Jude! What a one. You ask him for a stick or so of mesquite wood, let him see your electric bill, give him a little paper flag just to show you didn't forget him — the next thing you know he gives you a swimming pool. Ah, Jude. We have to try so hard to understand what a saint has in his mind sometimes. We have to realize that he knows more than we ourselves do what it is we need.

Going home on the bus Mrs. Domingo is very quiet and Mrs. Reyes does not interrupt her thoughts. Mrs. Domingo gets off the bus three blocks ahead of her regular stop in order to pass by the saint. And when she stands directly in front of him she bends forward to peer into his blue plaster eyes. But there is no flicker there. No sign passes between them as each one gazes straight ahead at the Kon Tiki swimming pool folder which Mrs. Domingo holds stiffly out in front of her.

It is time to go home. She knows that Rose, her youngest daughter, is probably down the street at the B-29 bar but Mrs. Domingo would never think of going there. Besides, she isn't ready to tell anyone about the swimming pool yet. Maybe she won't say anything until tomorrow. Yes, that would be best. No need to blurt out everything you know, everything you think, everything you feel to the first person who will listen to you the way white people do. Mrs. Domingo has certain thoughts which will go unspoken all of her life . . . .

She turns west going a block out of her way to avoid the Chinese grocery store where she owes a two-months' bill. She walks slowly down the alley watching the sunset light the thousands of pieces of broken bottles which dot the vacant lot. Some of them have been there so long they have turned purple from the Arizona sun, but most of them are still clear jagged slivers of wine bottles, dark amber bits of beer bottles piercing the sandy earth. There are no whole bottles. If the poor wino who drained the last drop lacked the strength to throw it hard enough to break, that would be taken care of by passing children soon enough.

Mrs. Domingo stops at the edge of her own property and looks it over carefully, every weed, every little heap of wood, every broken toy. Near the street is a small adobe ruin, never finished, never roofed. No doors or windows or floors. Only the mud walls of what was supposed to have been three rooms. They call it The House anyway. For twenty-three years it has stood this way, washing away a little in every summer's rains, crumbling grain by grain under every gust of wind. Mrs. Domingo always thinks of The House when she hears rain at night. Hold up, you old walls. Hold up because someday we're going to get a roof over you yet.

Mrs. Domingo goes into The House and sits as she has so many times before on a stack of adobe bricks which have been piled up there in the front room for twenty-three years.

It had all been a possible hope then, more than a dream, for adobes are a firm earth-colored reality. The hand feels safe somehow touching adobes . . . better than brick or cement or wood. And it is good for a house to be made of earth, to keep the color of the earth forever, to have the smell of earth about it too.

Twenty-three years ago when Juan Domingo and his two brothers had finally saved enough money between them to pay a hundred dollars for a vacant lot, they had planned to build two houses. Two rooms each, possibly three. They made their own adobe bricks and the walls grew, but not fast enough.

When Juan Domingo died of tuberculosis — died in the city jail so they could never know what messages he might have left them — that was the end of the house too. They had taken his body in a borrowed truck out to the reservation village where he had been born and had put up a blue cross for him in a rocky little desert cemetery within sight of Baboquivari Mountain. They tied ribbons to the cross; and left a candle burning in a coffee can and when they got back to town that night a hard summer rain was already tearing at those walls. Water poured down where the roof should have been, lay in puddles in the dirt. The House looked thinner after every storm as though the walls, never having been a real house, wished to sink back to earth. Not even St. Jude could help, so they quit mentioning it to him.

30

Tonight Mrs. Domingo lets her hand move tenderly across the wall. Hold up, you old walls, she thinks out of habit.

Behind The House is a shower stall where a hose hangs down over a board. Then the outhouse. Then the place where they live. Juan Domingo had put it up just to give them a roof while they were making adobes for The House. They thought of it only as a temporary shelter then, like the summer shelters their families used to build on the reservation when they went to their fields or when they were picking sahuaro fruit. Those summer shelters, not much more than ramadas, were fresh-smelling and leafy and open to every small breeze. Mrs. Domingo remembers a house of tall bending ocotillo stalks, still green, still blooming long after the ocotillos were cut.

But this place in town is made of corrugated tin sheets and old boards picked up at the city dump. No portion of it is the same material which was nailed and wired together twenty-three years ago. As one piece of wood rots and falls, another takes its place. When a piece of tin goes to rust, another is thrust over it, perhaps with a square of heavy cardboard filling a space the new tin doesn't quite cover. Sometimes discarded signs are used. **NO PARKING. NO TRESPASSING. DANGER. HEAVY LOAD.** Over the years the messages change.

Inside, a dirt floor. The gas stove isn't being used now because the bill wasn't paid. Most of the space here is taken up by beds but there is one small table and three chairs, not enough for everyone to sit down at once unless they bring in the wooden boxes and the bench from outside.

There are several pictures hung high on the walls, a wedding picture and a color photograph of St. Francis Xavier. There is a cigar box nailed up over the door and in it are whatever papers seem important enough to save. Bills, mostly. Unpleasant notices from welfare, from unemployment, bills for cars long since repossessed, even advertisements for life insurance and burial plots if the envelope is marked **IMPORTANT**. Tomorrow Mrs. Domingo will tell her grandson to stand on a chair and put the Kon Tiki pool papers into the cigar box too. But tonight she doesn't mention it.

They sit outside until it is dark and the grandchildren and the dogs and the transistor radios are all home again.

In this house live Mrs. Domingo, her daughter Rose (unless she is staying with a man), and Rose's two children. Then there is an older daughter, Lupe, and her husband and their three children. They sleep in the yard now because it is summer. Maybe by fall they will be in a place of their own again. But now Lupe is sick . . . crazy sick, a sickness of the mind. Everybody knows how she was witched by a Mexican *bruja,* poor thing, an evil woman who is said to have her saints all turned to the wall. Everyone in the family has been trying to save a dime here and there so they can afford to take her somewhere for a cure or have a medicine man come into town from the reservation. If they can't afford anything better, they'll finally take her over to the county clinic.

Lupe is sleeping now but she will be awake soon. She roams the alleys and vacant lots at night, fearful, her mind full of terrifying dreams, fears, the cries of owls, the relentless knowledge of impending disaster. At night darkness keeps her awake. During the day she falls down on one of the mattresses in the yard and sleeps fitfully, her hands reaching out as she sleeps, her fists clenching.

"Grandma, listen. When she cooked she forgot to put the frijoles in. No beans. Just water, that's all."

"But we put the frijoles in when she was asleep. It was late though, so they're still hard."

The children are standing at the wood stove poking in the iron pot with spoons, testing the hard beans, spitting them out in the dirt, and laughing. Lupe's husband, Ignacio, is sitting on the ground carving a flute with his pocketknife. Mrs. Domingo sees in his eyes the soft look of wine and she glances around for the bottle. He follows her thoughts, sighs, and says, "It was for my sorrow." He nods in the direction of Lupe.

Mrs. Domingo makes tortillas, puts molasses and peanut butter and noodles — all free surplus foods from welfare — on the table in the kitchen. The children serve themselves and take their plates outside and sit in the dirt.

"The beans will be for tomorrow," Mrs. Domingo says. "And tomorrow we can make tacos too because I have money from the fair. We'll have meat."

After supper Mrs. Domingo walks around the outside of the tin house, all sides, trying to decide where to put the swimming pool. There is room, perhaps, between the alley and the outhouse. Or maybe they could move the woodpile closer to the fence. They could move the big iron washtubs too.

What's your suggestion, Jude?

When the Kon Tiki pool man arrives on Monday they bring the best chair out under the chinaberry tree for him to sit on. Even so, he looks ill at ease, keeps clearing his throat. Finally the children whisper, "Is that man okay?"

Mrs. Domingo has the second best chair. The others stand grouped around them, the older children holding the babies, Ignacio wearing his good wide-brimmed straw hat, Lupe from time to time lifting her head from the mattress to look at them. Rose is home too with her friend, Maria

33

Vasquez, and they stand behind the children. Everyone is very serious at the sight of so many papers in the man's briefcase. He hands them to Mrs. Domingo. She looks and passes them on to the children, to Ignacio, to Rose, to Maria, everyone except Lupe.

"Now then," the man says, "I'd better have a look at your property line . . . water hook up . . . water meter . . . ."

One of the boys points to the faucet over by the fence.

"The meter," the man says. "Just show me the meter."

"But why would we need a meter?" Mrs. Domingo asks.

The man looks hopefully toward the boy who had shown him the faucet. "You know where the meter is?"

"We don't have it." The boy is proud that he knows about such things. "That water comes from a neighbor. But we have a hose for when we want it to go to the shower."

The man rubs his head from time to time.

Mrs. Domingo tells him, "It's not so bad. Not much trouble to take a bucket into the house. Really."

Now the man is striding back and forth kicking up dust. He stops in front of the faucet, looks around at the little group of faces. "We may have a problem here."

"And what problem is that?" Mrs. Domingo asks.

So he has to tell her. "Lady, you don't even have indoor plumbing! Look, you're not hooked up to the city water pipes. You —"

He opens his folder of papers again and in a strained, tired voice speaks of such things as the electric filter system, the distance of city water pipes, the number of gallons required to fill a pool. No one knows what he is saying as he points first to one page and then another.

When he stops talking there is a long pause. Finally he comes over to them and starts again. "It's next to impossible. . . ."

Mrs. Domingo does not look as disappointed as the man does. "Tell us this," she says. "You can dig the hole all right, can't you?"

"Yes," he says.

"Okay," Mrs. Domingo says. "Just tell them to dig the hole and plaster it. We don't care about the water and the electricity and all that."

"Lady, you want a swimming pool with no water in it?"

"I want steps down in."

"But no water?"

"That's right."

"Oh, God," the man says.

"I want the pretty blue around the edge."

"But no water?"

"No." Mrs. Domingo is looking off toward the mountains because she does not wish to look at the Kon Tiki pool man any longer. She does not wish to argue about such a simple thing.

But the pool man doesn't give up easily. "Lady," he says, "maybe they could work out some other prize or something."

"Why would I want some other prize? I want my swimming pool." Mrs. Domingo's voice is very low but she lifts her hand to show that her mind is made up.

"Maybe a cash prize?"

"Maybe so," Ignacio and Rose agree. "Maybe that."

But Mrs. Domingo shakes her head and no one else says anything. They sense that she has her own reasons and they know that it is her prize after all. Besides, she's old enough to have some wisdom. Now they nod and wait for the Kon Tiki man to get into his car and drive away. None of them even walks out to the street to watch him drive away. Instead, they wait clustered around Mrs. Domingo.

As soon as he is out of sight she begins to smile.

"Would St. Jude be stupid enough to give us a puddle of cold water when what we need is a house?"

"Not him," they agree.

"He does what he can," Mrs. Domingo explains to them. "He couldn't give us adobes and glass windows for The House but he has done the best he could."

So they understand. "The pool. Sure," Rose says.

Mrs. Domingo grins. "Wouldn't he have thought we were the dumb ones if we had put water in it?"

They walk over to the side of the tin house where Ignacio has drawn the shape of a pool in the dirt with a stick.

"We'll have the ramada builder come and put a roof over it," Mrs. Domingo says. "A good roof."

She goes to the wood stove, pours herself some black coffee, brings the big tin cup and sits down beside the mark which shows where the swimming pool is to be.

CHAPTER 4

MARIA VASQUEZ

It's a long walk to the welfare office, and Maria is always glad of that. If it were just around the corner and you knew when you started that you'd be there in five minutes, who would have the courage to go at all? But when the distance is great you can always hope that something will change the shape of the day before you get there . . . .

Maria has already begun that walk three times this week. Once she turned aside at the B-29 bar. Once she felt strange pains grasping at her stomach and had to stop at Mrs. Fuentes' house for herbs to make a broth. And the other time she arrived late enough that the door was locked.

The first eight or ten blocks are always all right. You see the dark soft faces you know — whether or not you remember their names. You see adobe houses you have lived in at other times little better or worse than this time. Everything is familiar: the naked babies, the little girls wearing somebody's long loose give-away dresses, the old people with their chairs on the sidewalk, boys leaning against cars that do not run. You know the smells of the houses, the mesquite cooking fires, the chile, the coffee, the strong soap in the washtubs.

You even recognize the polite and persistent young Anglo men taking their Mormon books and magazines from door to door. You recognize their black suits, their polished shoes, their shiny narrow black ties. Protestants sometimes let them in. Catholics, never.

Here any house with green vines clinging to the walls and tremendous floppy ferns in tin wash buckets and pink geraniums in coffee cans will be a house where Mexicans live. Mexicans or Yaqui Indians from Mexico. They too love ferns and flowers and they enclose their homes with high board fences held up by generations of summer vines, old and new tangled together, strong as wire.

Only Papago Indian houses grow out of a bare dirt yard. Maybe one mesquite tree. Maybe a clump of corn around by the back door. But almost never those masses of leaves and flowers. More often you'll see a little heap of pretty rocks, blue copper ore or twisting concretions or ancient grinding stones, *manos* and *metates* from the reservation. Here a yard may be raked or swept for special days. A Papago admires an open sandy area swept flat and hard. After centuries of surviving in the desert, Papago people have their own way of seeing earth and rocks and plants. Even now in town something stops them from pouring out water just for the pleasure of a green leaf.

But this familiar world fades as Maria walks north. The closer she comes to the Anglo part of town the more she feels ill at ease, different, dark, heavy.

This time she has brought her three oldest girls along for company.

Now she warns them, "Whatever they ask, be careful not to tell."

"Like what, Mama?"

"Like do I drink beer . . . ."

"Sure you drink beer, Mama." They giggle.

"Well, don't tell. Or like do men come to see me sometime."

"Sure they do. Sometime."

"Just don't tell." Maria herself doesn't know what they might ask. You never can guess.

They walk in silence for a time. "Don't men come to see white ladies?" Amelia asks. "Don't they like to kiss white ladies?"

Anna, the oldest, says, "Not just kiss, stupid. Have babies."

Amelia nods. "Well, don't they like that?"

"Not the ladies at welfare," Anna tells her.

And that reminds Maria of something else. "Listen," she says, "if they ask you what do you want to be when you grow up, you better say nurses. Nurses or teachers. Either one."

But as it turns out, no one asks the girls anything at all. They walk into the welfare office and sit very quietly on the edge of their chairs.

After a while the woman at the reception desk motions to Maria. The girls watch their mother, slow step by step, lifting her dusty shoes across the polished red tile squares of the floor.

"Didn't you read the sign?"

Maria shakes her head.

The woman points with a pencil. **PUBLIC ASSISTANCE APPLICANTS ARE REQUESTED NOT TO BRING CHILDREN TO THIS OFFICE.**

Maria reads it carefully, looks questioningly at the children. Anna, Amelia, and Jane go over to look at the sign.

The woman at the desk has gone back to her typing but the children remain standing. "Would it be okay if they don't sit?" Maria whispers.

Finally the woman says, "It *is* a rule, so we all have to abide by it. Now—"

"But why?" Maria asks. Usually you don't ask white people why, but this time she is truly curious. It would be interesting to know. "What would it hurt?"

The woman types a few more words and then she stops and looks at Maria again and sighs. "For heaven's sake," she says, "do you want your children to know all your problems? Certain things should be absolutely private between you and your case worker. Certain things are simply not for children to hear. For their own good."

The children's eyes ask, what things? Maria too wonders. Papago children go to dances and funerals and fiestas along with the adults. And with six or seven people sleeping in the same room, there's not much privacy even in bed. Not many secrets from the children . . . .

Besides that, Papago children are used to making their own decisions. They say whether or not they are going to school, or whether they will go to the county hospital to get a cut foot bandaged, or whether they will stay in town or go back to a grandmother in her reservation village . . . .

Wasn't Maria supposed to have let them know they didn't have a house anymore? Or is it something else that children are not supposed to know? What secrets would she keep from them and then tell to a social worker? None, none.

"Don't we already know?" Amelia asks, whispering.

"I do," says Jane.

"Don't tell," Anna reminds them. "Just shut up."

They stand by the door, a dark silent cluster.

"They could sit on the curb outside, I guess," Maria says. "But so many cars."

"Well, you should have thought of that before you brought them, shouldn't you. It's not *my* rule, you know."

Without saying anything else, the children go outside and sit on the steps. Maria moves slowly across the room to a chair and waits, her hands folded in her lap, her eyes open but blank. Her gaze is far away, remote, not bound by the green walls of the welfare office.

A few black women read torn limp magazines as they wait. The Mexican women too if they read English. Anyway they look at the pictures, talk, move their hands. Only Indian women sit. Simply sit.

After an hour Maria hears her name called and goes into a small cubicle where Mrs. Agnes Waterman is taking papers from a file cabinet. They know each other; it was Mrs. Waterman who had once told Maria not under *any* circumstances to have another baby, so Maria has never given them Carmen's name. She will remember not to mention her today.

Now from habit Mrs. Waterman glances at her client's belly. Pregnant or just putting on weight? Maria feels that glance as she has so many times before, but she gives no sign. Is this one of the secrets you are supposed to share with your case worker . . . even the secrets inside your body?

She remembers once hearing a white man say, "Them teenage Indian girls is good lookers. But Christ, they get big so fast . . . ."

She knows that white women starve themselves to stay bony and ugly. But you can't get thin on beans and tortillas. And anyway Indian men like the roundness of a woman, the softness, the fullness. Not a skinny fence post . . . .

"Same address, Mrs. Vasquez?"

Maria hesitates, hoping there is no rule in the book against sleeping outside.

"You haven't moved, have you?"

"They boarded up that place the other day. The health department did."

"And your new address?"

"Well, I'm paid up until Friday so we just live in the back yard . . . there by the alley."

As soon as she says it, Maria knows it was a mistake. The look on Mrs. Waterman's face tells her that this is not the secret to share with your case worker.

"The back yard of a condemned house? That's where you keep those children? That's where you *live?*"

"Well, it's so hot this month . . . better to be out than inside."

With her pen, Mrs. Waterman is tapping a large book which must surely be the book of rules.

"Let's think about it together, Mrs. Vasquez. Because if the health department condemned that house, they must have had a good reason, mustn't they?"

"I guess so." Maria hopes Mrs. Waterman won't ask her what that reason might be.

Mrs. Waterman nods. "They're only trying to make sure children have suitable homes, not trying to make trouble for anyone. Now let me put it this way. Do you think the alley is a suitable home?"

Maria waits. You learn to wait. You suspend yourself high above the sound of their words, a dark bird lifted motionless in the sky. And time passes.

"And where's your husband, Mrs. Vasquez?"

"Gone. Maybe gone to pick melons. Maybe lettuce. Just trying to find work somewhere . . . ."

She does not look at Mrs. Waterman, and her voice stays very low as she speaks. No ups and downs, no special emphasis, no whining, no pleading either.

But when Agnes Waterman is upset she can't keep her voice that steady. It goes up now.

"Where? Where is he?"

"I don't know. He didn't write." She looks down, folds her handkerchief, unfolds it, smooths it, folds it with slow, slow fingers.

"You'll have to sign the nonsupport charge. You've been deserted."

"But I'm not deserted," Maria says.

Mrs. Waterman shakes her head. Her voice sounds tired. How many women has she said the same thing to today? How many has she failed to convince?

"All you women," she says. "Doesn't it make you angry?"

"At him?"

"Listen, if a father isn't supporting his children, then he's guilty of nonsupport. It's just that simple, Mrs. Vasquez.

That's why you have to sign the charges this time or we can't legally help you at all."

Maria only folds the handkerchief again. Things always seem so distinct to Anglos, the lines so clearly drawn, everything pulled apart, separated into squares, written in a book of rules . . . and written in English.

"Believe me, I understand your feeling, Mrs. Vasquez, but it's the only thing to do."

Yet the welfare people almost never persuade Papago women to sign those papers claiming that they have been deserted by their men. "Yes, I'll be down . . . Yes, I'll put my name on the paper next week. . . ." But they don't come. What kind of woman signs a paper against a man so they can lock him up in jail? What kind of woman doesn't remember something that keeps her from putting her name on that paper?

Signing any paper is a serious and solemn matter anyway. A paper is so much a white man's object, always signed with some white person watching you, telling you which line to put your name on, making you feel the power of the paper.

"Oh yes," Maria says, "maybe next week. I'll sign it then if he's not back . . . ."

But in her mind it's, don't worry, Joe. St. Jude take care of you. Somebody give you a swig from his bottle of tokay. And wherever you are, stay out of jail if you can . . . .

But how can you tell Mrs. Waterman that bad luck is to blame, not poor fat wino Joe Vasquez. An Indian can say, "Well, this is the turn life has taken." It's like saying, "It rained or it didn't rain. We're out of frijoles." But Mrs. Waterman has to have three copies of a paper saying who is to blame.

"You women get stuck with the problems — stuck with feeding a house full of children — and you let the men run free," she says. "Honestly, I don't understand it." Her face is flushed. Maybe she really does wish to understand.

But Maria doesn't try to explain anything.

"And I have to warn you, Mrs. Vasquez, if there's any other man living with you, then he is responsible for the full support of those children. Now if you get help from the county, remember, there can be *no* man spending the night in that house . . . ."

Maria pushes her fingers together, feels her body tighten, doesn't say a word.

Do white people really think it is so evil to lie down with a man? Of all sins, loving a man—whether it's in bed or in some clump of weeds on the hard earth—seems the one most worth risking God's anger for . . . or even the anger of a social worker.

"Oh, no. No man," Maria says. She can't imagine Mrs. Waterman naked with a man. She can't imagine Mrs. Waterman crying for a man after he is gone either, lying awake, remembering . . . .

Suddenly, she almost smiles at the woman across the desk, the woman with the book of rules. Not quite though. Mrs. Waterman has never seen Maria either smile or show anger. In fact, she has never seen any of her Indian clients weep. White women, black women, Mexicans—they all occasionally cry or curse or scream out in frustration and anger. Not Indians. And so Mrs. Waterman can't possibly know that right now Maria is damp all over, her insides shaking.

Mrs. Waterman is writing something. "Here's an emergency grocery order," she says.

"No money to rent another place, I guess?"

"Let me put it this way, Mrs. Vasquez. We're supposed to be helping mothers run homes for their children. But if you don't even have a home for them, then we aren't authorized to assist you. Now as a resident of this county, you'll have to have an address first. You come back when you have an address."

Maria nods and gets up.

"And Mrs. Vasquez . . . ."

"Yes?"

"Remember, we'll need birth certificates for the children. Either that or baptismal certificates."

"But I don't have them."

"We have to have proof of birth. It's a regulation."

Maria hesitates, decides to speak. "Couldn't I bring them in . . . the children? You could see that they were born, each one."

"No, I'll have to have a paper for them."

Maria shrugs. Of course they always want a paper. Some kind of paper. Leaning against the door now, waiting to be dismissed, she thinks how many centuries her people lived out there in the desert without papers . . . remembers once seeing a calendar stick carved with notches and circles and dots and zig-zag lines which told the entire history of her village, its battles, floods, droughts, even a meteor that fell.

"And one thing more, Mrs. Vasquez."

"Yes?"

"I want to advise you — and this isn't meant as criticism — but if you honestly want to improve your life, then you'd better set some goals and start planning a little, not just drifting along like some . . . some . . . mouse."

Maria smiles at that mouse. She likes him better than anything else around here.

"So you go on home, Mrs. Vasquez, and make some plans. And I hope you'll be realistic enough to admit you've been deserted and that any man who deserts his family belongs in jail."

"Okay . . . well . . . ."

She manages to get out of the building and when she does she sinks down on the front steps where her children are waiting. She has to squint, but it is good to be outside again.

"Did they ask you about drinking beer?" Anna says. "Or going to dances?"

"Not that," Maria says.

"What?"

"They want me to sign a paper against your daddy."

"Don't do it." They all say it. And Amelia, the five-year-old, reminds them, "He hates jail, our daddy. He hates the cage they put him in."

"He does," Anna says.

They start back toward the condemned house, going through the alley this time, kicking up small clouds of dust as they walk.

For the last four years an abandoned car has sat in this alley just behind the house. Each year it sinks deeper into the earth, wheels gone, fenders gone, motor and hood and lights gone too. But the doors still open and close, and the steering wheel is there. The car is almost never empty. Usually some small dark child is at the wheel with some sleeping wino for his passenger.

"Where you want to go to, Mr. Martinez?"

Maybe the man will lift his head, maybe not. "You know the way to Coyote village? You know that road?"

"I know all the roads."

ZOOM. ZOOM.

Today Errol Flynn Vasquez is the driver. Carmen is on the seat beside him, and in the back is the old man everyone calls the Ramada Builder. His names is Jesus Gomez, and if you want a ramada built you send for him even though you could build it well enough yourself. The thing is, he likes to build ramadas. If you can give him a dime and a plate of frijoles for his trouble, he is happy.

This one isn't a wino, but he's funny in his mind. If he wants a place to sleep some rainy night, there's not an Indian family around who would turn him down.

Now Maria and the three older girls come up to the car where Errol Flynn is going ZOOM ZOOM and Carmen is sitting quietly beside him and the Ramada Builder is smiling in the back seat. The girls all pile in.

Maria knows the Ramada Builder has been with some of the Indians who drifted over to Yuma to the melon fields, and she asks him through the window, "Did you see Joe Vasquez over where you went?"

Jesus Gomez smiles and nods.

"Where was he? In jail or out?"

But time is always mixed up in the Ramada Builder's mind so he frowns, puzzled. Maria doesn't ask again. She knows the question will stay in his mind and in a week or so he may think of the answer. Sometimes he remembers in a day, sometimes it's thirty years.

The Ramada Builder remembers something else though. "I come back to town," he says, "because I got to make a ramada over at Elma Domingo's. They're digging a house in the ground over there. Pretty good house."

"It's a swimming pool," Errol Flynn tells him.

"Well, I come back to put a roof over it," the Ramada Builder says proudly. "Me."

Maria goes on into the back yard and makes a mesquite fire in the wood stove, starts patting out the tortillas, stirs the beans, but all the time she has Mrs. Waterman's white face in her mind, still feels closed in by the green walls of the welfare office.

She moves slowly, unhurriedly about the yard. The sun goes down and the earth cools enough so that now they can take off their shoes.

Toward evening as the lights go on up and down the street, Maria lights the kerosene lamp and sets it on one of the cardboard boxes.

She likes lights, electric lights. In her reservation home there had been candles and lamps. A pan of hot coals was carried in at night when it was cold. You went to sleep watching that faint glow under the ashes.

She remembers the first time she saw the lights of Tucson from afar as they came driving in a pickup truck from the reservation, came up the rise of the mountains and looked over the valley.

Maria had been fourteen and she had never before imagined a sight of such sudden beauty. She didn't say anything then, of course, just sucked in her breath and leaned her head out of the truck in the wind. She saw in those lights a new life in the greater world. Music, fiestas, saints, days, dancing. She didn't know why else electric lights should burn . . . .

Now she wonders if one of the lights she saw that night might have come from the small high windows of the B-29 bar. Perhaps one from St. Jude. One from the welfare office.

Well, tonight she wants a brighter light than Jude's blue candles. Tonight it has to be the fifty-watt bulb hanging from its dirty cord in the center of the B-29. She puts on dark red lipstick, looking at the flat planes of her face in a jagged piece of broken mirror which they have propped in the mesquite tree, brushes her thick black hair.

"Are you going to drink beer, Mama?"

"A little."

But Amelia, the one who likes to have things arranged in her mind, turns her face up to Maria. "We better get a house tomorrow. What if it rains?"

They look at the sky. The Ramada Builder has climbed out of the car and followed them to the plate of warm tortillas.

"We could sit in the car," Errol Flynn says.

The Ramada Builder has an idea too. "If it rains, I make a good ramada and you run get under it."

But Amelia still isn't satisfied. "The rain would blow in. Anyway we don't have posts to build it."

They are all sitting on the ground eating beans rolled up in large soft tortillas, all looking east where lightning touches the sky over the mountains.

"Mama, you better think about it while you're drinking beer."

"Okay," Maria promises. But she won't think about it tonight. You don't go to the B-29 to think of rain coming down on your cardboard boxes or your children. You go to the B-29 because it's as close as you can come to the promise of those first electric lights. And because there is music that doesn't stop, good loud music. And another thing too. You go to the B-29 because everybody there knows something that Mrs. Agnes Waterman doesn't know. They know that rain or no rain, house or no house, man or no man, you just keep on breathing. You don't have to write it down on a piece of white paper first or make everybody sign it to show that you have a plan.

Have you a plan, Mrs. Vasquez? Oh, sure, I plan to stay alive. Where do I sign up?

All the way to the B-29 Maria thinks of Mrs. Waterman's gold glasses, her pearl pin. Pictures herself saying, "Here's a certain secret I'll tell you, something those kids of mine don't know a thing about . . . ."

But she can't finish the scene because she can't decide on the secret. She thinks of it until the door of the B-29 opens and she wraps herself in its Indian sounds.

CHAPTER 5

THE RAMADA BUILDER

He isn't sure about his name. It's whatever anyone wants to call him. Jesus Gomez. Dumb Indian Bastard. Ramada Builder. Crazy One. Poco Loco. Long ago it was Little Brother, That One.

When he talks to people he always waits to find out what they are going to call him. Then that's his name.

Ramada Builder is the one he likes best. Call him that and he smiles showing his crooked broken teeth, twisting his head to squint at the speaker.

That name means working two days, maybe three for an Indian — not a white man. He likes that because Indians never shout at him. They don't get mad if he makes some little mistake . . . if he gets the roof of the ramada too low, something like that.

Everybody knows that if you want a ramada you send word to Jesus Gomez and he will walk away from whatever job he is doing and bring his own axe and hammer and stand at your door nodding and smiling. He doesn't want to wait until tomorrow. He wants to start now.

Ramada Builder. When he hears that name he knows it means having someone take him out to the desert in a pickup truck or a wagon to chop mesquite posts for a ramada — four posts if it is a small one, six posts if it is to be larger, good straight posts (as straight as you can get from those twisting mesquite trees), posts forked at the top to hold the cross pieces. Four or six. These are the only numbers he knows, the only ones he needs to know. He has to count them on his dark stubby fingers. Sometimes he forgets where he has left a post and walks over two or three rocky hills looking for it and finally has to cut another, but it is good work anyway. Happy work. He doesn't mind.

Ramada Builder. It means using an axe, raising your arms high and coming down with all your strength against the wood, making the chips fly. That's something the Ramada Builder can do as well as anyone; he's strong.

Ramada Builder. It means digging post holes. He loves to have children watch him work. He chuckles as he brings up shovelfuls of earth from darkness into light, throwing the earth into a little heap, later pressing it down around the posts, feeling it cool against his hands. And then some kind of roof, maybe long sahuaro ribs or ocotillos, sometimes just greasewood branches for shade. It is a pleasant thing to do, making that patch of shade. The best part of any house whether it's on the reservation or in town . . . the place you sleep on summer nights, the place you come back to on summer days when it's too hot to go inside, too hot to move.

Women always seem to be cooking while the men are building ramadas, and they will give you a plate of beans and a tortilla. Sometimes money too. A nickel or a dime or a quarter.

The Ramada Builder doesn't like paper money. He likes coins, any kind, but especially nickels and quarters. He wants several of them, enough to feel them moving in his levi pocket, clinking against the small beautiful blue and green stones he always carries with him. He won't work for a man who doesn't give him some of those coins every day. He can't wait a week.

He doesn't have to live in town. Relatives in two different villages on the reservation will take him in any time, but he never stays there long. He likes to work, to be with other men who are working. Then he feels like a man too. If he isn't doing man's work, he forgets that he isn't a child.

Sometimes he goes as far from home as Yuma. He picks melons or oranges. He chops cotton, works in the lettuce fields. But if night comes and they haven't given him a handful of money he won't stay in the camp. His eyes will fill with tears and he'll start walking down the road no matter what time it is, no matter how dark.

The other men try to tell him he lets the boss cheat him when he takes two or three nickels for a day's work, but he only shakes his head. He knows how much he needs. He knows how much a piece of candy costs.

There is one place in Tucson he likes so much he will work free for anyone who takes him there. That's the city dump. A place of mystery and joy and wonder. He often dreams of it at night and laughs aloud.

Sometimes a man who sells rags and paper and scrap metal comes looking for him in a rusted blue pickup truck with broken springs. When the Ramada Builder sees that truck he knows they'll be going to the dump. As soon as they get near enough to see the smoke coming over the hill, the Ramada Builder's heart begins thumping and he smiles and nods. "Good place to come to. Nice place to come to, no?"

"You bet your life," the man always says. "Just take it easy."

CITY PROPERTY, the sign reads. **SANITARY LAND-FILL. SLOW.**

The dust on the road is powdery. It rises high as they pass and the Ramada Builder likes the motion of it.

This isn't desert anymore. Not a cactus. Not a greasewood bush in sight. The landscape here changes day by day as the great lumbering machines open the earth to make new pits for masses of throwaway treasures. Here the raw earth, newly turned by bulldozers, loses its permanency, its strength. It shifts, becomes soft, sinks down. When the heavy foot of the Ramada Builder touches this flat barren sand he misses the feel of hard real earth. This is like walking over some new world. Wasn't the earth soft when

Earthmaker with his great brown hands formed the first world for the Papago people to walk on? Soft as this . . . .

There are two groups of people at the dump: those who come to throw away the things they no longer want, and those who come to take those same things away. There is an even exchange here. The leavings of some become the prizes of others.

Every time a truck or car or station wagon curves its way down the dirt road, the scavengers watch carefully to see what the cargo is. *My God, look at them good chairs . . . Look at that lumber . . . Damn, not a thing but junk. Just my luck, man. Junk.*

You have to work fast to keep ahead of the bulldozers. You run if you have to, but it's best when you can take your time poking into the mounds of discarded objects, waiting for a truck to arrive and then going over to help the driver unload. That gives you first choice.

You don't fight over things. You wait your turn. You go early. You stay late. You even learn to recognize which people's garbage is so full of still-usable treasures that you run for it. You learn which things you can sell somewhere for a dime. If you're lucky you'll find papers and magazines that arrive at the dump already tied in bundles. Maybe a car seat you can take home and put in the back yard. Maybe some corrugated sheet metal or pieces of peeling plywood that will do for patching a wall or a roof.

The Ramada Builder knows everyone. He smiles and his big head bobs loosely to the old man sitting on a stained mattress thumbing through *Life* magazine, to the black children trying to ride a scooter with no wheels. He'd like to ride it too, but no. He has a job today. Has to work with men today.

There's the woman with the red hair. He has seen her here a dozen times, has stood still for minutes at a time gazing across the field at that flaming hair. Red, the color of copper tubing, finer than the tiny wires in electric coils, metallic, shiny as a beetle's wing. She's so beautiful. Prettier than anybody. Prettier than the painted statue of the Blessed Virgin even. He can't move his eyes away from her red hair blazing in the sun like a neon sign. Doesn't really see the rest of her.

She may be old. He can't tell that. But look at her wheel that little wagon across the sand. She always has it with her. Today it is heaped with cracked, torn tarpaper. The Ramada Builder likes tarpaper himself. She's smart, he thinks. Smart to find all that before anyone else.

She's the one who settles arguments here, tells people to keep out of the way of the bulldozers, shouts at the kids when they kick up too much dust.

He spots a straw hat. A good straw hat, wide brimmed, only a little part of the straw unraveling. Maybe one little hole in it. A good hat. The Ramada Builder runs for it, but his short legs move so clumsily here in the soft earth that the children get to the hat first and grab it up and take turns pulling it down over their faces.

"My good hat," he yells, but they only laugh at him. He sits down in the dirt and holds out his hands toward the hat. No use running now. But the red-haired woman moves into the circle and just lifts her thumb in the direction of the Ramada Builder. "Give it to him, stupid," she says to the boy who is wearing the hat. That's all. She doesn't have to say anything else. The Ramada Builder gets up off the ground grinning and grabs the hat and the children throw a couple of handfuls of dirt after him, but nobody tries to get the hat back when he picks it up and pulls it down over his own matted hair.

"Hey, you, Ramada Builder. I didn't cart you out here to stand around. What the hell you think I brought you here for?"

The Ramada Builder always wants to do the right thing. But sometimes he forgets. Now he hurries, gathers armloads of paper, of metal, anything they can sell for scrap.

Works two or three hours, rummaging through heaps of junk, finally has a great pile of things to throw in the back of the truck.

But a white car wheels in. Everything stops.

"Shit," the red-haired woman calls out. "It's the cops."

Look how fast she sees things, the Ramada Builder thinks.

Like a movie film suddenly beginning to run backwards, the poor reverse their armload of lumber and wire. People who have been loading old tires and repairable trellises into their cars now begin slowly to unload them. Even the Ramada Builder has learned what to do. It is time for the poor to pretend they are the rich, that they are discarding, not collecting. Nobody knows just why it is legal to dump, not legal to take. Just one of the rules white people make. Even so, they all play the game with skill. The Ramada Builder chuckles as he throws tin and cardboard and wire out of the truck.

The police car makes one slow swing around the loop. They have never arrested anyone here for scavenging and the people sense that the police have to do their duty by driving past just as the poor do their duty by throwing things out of their cars.

The white police car disappears in a cloud of dust. Now they all begin reloading their cars, their trucks. They're used to it.

After he has worked all afternoon for the man who brought him here, the Ramada Builder still doesn't want to leave.

"Come on, man. We got to go."

"Not yet."

"Come on. I got a dime for you."

The Ramada Builder grins and nods, holds out his hand, but he keeps looking back at the flat open land, land still erupting with prizes.

"Somebody maybe give me a ride back. After while."

So he stays. Doesn't have to hurry now that he isn't working for anyone. Now he can please himself. He finds a broken rake. Everybody here walks with some kind of stick to pry into mounds, to sort, to dig.

The Ramada Builder is unbelievably happy. He whistles through his broken teeth as he walks among acres of rusted chicken wire, bed springs, lawn furniture now only twisted aluminum, lawn furniture festooned with plastic, bamboo draperies hanging in strips, odd lengths of hose, worn-out electric motors, car seats, sofa springs, gutted overstuffed chairs, mildewed clothing, rotted fence posts, plastic buckets, fenders, bumpers, hedge clippings, palm fronds, toilet seats, picture frames.

Here is a Christmas tree still trailing tinsel, old carpets, rubber pads, broken mirrors, plastic toys, burned pans, shower curtains, thin stiff brooms, rakes, license plates, plastic ice chests, boxes of jar lids, *Readers Digests,* single shoes, boots, cans of dry paint, lumber full of rusted nails, chair legs, cactus, lamp shades, ironing boards, old letters still held together with rubber bands, cancelled checks, broken bricks, dolls with no legs, glass jars of rancid grease, coat hangers, a wreath tied with a wide red ribbon. Beautiful. Beautiful. All of it. Like a dream.

Of course, everything is broken, but even so . . . .

The Ramada Builder can't tell time. If the sun is hot, he calls it day. If it's dark, night. But how many days and nights and how many summers and how many cold times has he known twist and circle in his head. Time does not divide his life into parts for him. There is no long ago. No someday. Now is all he knows.

Today he has stayed late at the dump, whistling, chuckling, murmuring to himself in soft fluid Papago words. He looks up suddenly and finds that it is dark and he is alone. Remembers that he was going to ask somebody for a ride back to the highway, but there is nobody left to ask.

A cat comes stepping daintily over a pile of bottles, sits down and watches the Ramada Builder as he peers into the thin summer darkness still searching for somebody who will give him a ride.

After a while the Ramada Builder knows it is too late. *Okay. I live here now. Maybe so.*

He lies down with his head on a tire. *Good place to live.* He wishes that smart red-haired woman would come live here too. Well, maybe she will. Nobody but them picking things up at night when the others have gone. Maybe a little fire when it gets cold. Maybe build a ramada with scraps of lumber. Yes, even that. For her.

He becomes aware of a light, a red-orange glow coming from one of the great open pits sunk into the earth. Flames twist, pull the night into them, grow larger, whisper, yelp. Orange clouds of smoke billow upward, cover the world.

Jesus Gomez flattens himself on the ground, burrows down into the papers, the wire, the tires. He whimpers, yet he cannot look away.

The mystery, the wonder of fire at night overpowers him. The color, the motion, the hiss of it fills him with such terror that his mouth is dry, his hands wet. Is it God? St. Francis maybe? A witch fire? The hell the priest speaks of? Even a sign from the Blessed Virgin? He works to bring one hand up from the dirt and crosses himself, says out loud, "I'll be good." Too bad he can't remember the words for Hail Mary.

The smell of burning debris fills his nostrils, makes his nose run, makes his eyes hurt. He spits.

The cat moves against him, grey as smoke, and they hunch together in the darkness, both watching the motion of the flames until one of the big dump trucks comes down the road. Then the cat runs, turns into night. The Ramada Builder stays flat against the earth until the truck lights pass. Then he crawls slowly, stretching his legs until they will move for him again, and he too begins running through the soft dirt, through the rubble, back toward the highway.

It's a long way to town. He runs and then walks, always toward the light. It takes all night. By dawn he is panting and gasping at Elma Domingo's house. Maybe he sleeps. They find him crouched by the old adobe walls when they come outside to wash.

"What's the matter with you?" the children ask. "You hiding from the cops?"

He hesitates, hangs his big dusty head. "Not cops. No, not cops."

"Who then?"

"A bunch of kids. Them mean kids threw rocks at me. Chased me. Threw rocks." He holds out his arms. "Made me all bloody, them rocks."

The children look but there is no blood. Just dirt. Mrs. Domingo comes out and the Ramada Builder tells her, too, still hiding behind the crumbling adobe walls, afraid.

But she has heard it before. She knows how time comes back in waves that cross his mind and fade and then return. Twenty years. Forty years. Yesterday. Today. She doesn't try to tell him that it was long ago those rocks sailed through the air at him. She just goes back into the house and brings out a dipper of water and a tortilla wrapped around a spoonful of beans, hands it to him, and finally says, "Listen, we got to have a ramada builder here at this place. We got to have a roof over the swimming pool."

"Okay," he says, still looking for blood on his arms. "I can do that. Me."

Then he begins to grin and finally he comes out from behind the adobes. "Today," he says.

CHAPTER 6

Maria Vasquez

For four nights now Maria has awakened before dawn believing there is a man near her. She turns and opens her arms and feels her belly come alive.

But there isn't any man here. She's on the mattress in the yard and the baby, Carmen, is beside her. Errol Flynn usually rolls off the mattress in the night and sleeps flat as a lizard against the earth. That's where he is now.

Maria sits up and puts her feet in the warm summer dirt, looks at the stars. Her insides can't be wrong. The feeling is too strong for that. And having it four nights in a row — four, the magic number for Papagos — that makes it certain.

Good luck or bad . . . a man can be either. All you can tell is that the path of your fate is changing. All you can do is wait for it to happen.

She drifts back to the edge of sleep, closes her eyes, keeps the thought of a man close against her in the darkness.

Maybe this one will stay with me and love me and my life will change. My life will take shape. Movies on Saturday nights. Mass on Sunday mornings. Trips to the reservation for feast days and dances and celebrations . . . .

You can't let yourself really hope for such good luck. You'd better keep such thoughts from coming too close. You don't quite finish thinking them because it's bad luck to expect too much. Who do you think you are?

When the sky turns its first pale orange in the east Maria is already putting a few small sticks of mesquite wood in the stove to make a pot of coffee.

As she moves about the yard barefooted, faded yellow dress hanging open, pinned in two or three places, she thinks of that social worker: "You'd better get yourself a plan, Mrs. Vasquez." Well, okay, Mrs. Agnes Waterman, you can write it down on all your papers. Maria Vasquez has got a plan now. She plans to have a man around again. Write it on three pieces of your paper, please . . . .

Maria takes an empty five-pound lard can and walks across the alley to get water from the hose by Mrs. Domingo's fence. Here people are still asleep outside and the children and the dogs are curled up on blankets down inside the empty swimming pool.

When she gets back with the water her own children are beginning to wake and she tells them, "I got a job to go to today."

"A white lady?" Anna asks.

"You better go," Amelia says. "We need the money to get a house."

But Errol Flynn just laughs at Amelia. "That's not enough money for a house, is it, Mama?"

Maria shakes her head.

"It's okay for food, not a house," Errol Flynn says. "Me, I'd rather have food."

"Meat," says Jane. "Meat and chile and oranges and candy."

They have last night's beans wrapped in tortillas and they all drink a little coffee with canned milk and sugar.

Before Maria leaves she hangs the can of water in the mesquite tree, tells them, "Listen, if white people come around, don't say we live here. Just say we left some of our stuff."

"We could tell them we're going back to the reservation," Amelia says. "How about that?"

Maria shrugs. Whenever things are bad she talks about going back to the reservation. She's probably said it a hundred times: "Gonna take you kids back to Ventana where my aunt is . . . maybe over by Big Fields. Build us our own house out there."

But the children know they aren't going back. Half the time the Indians who've moved into Tucson will say to each other, "Don't know what I'm doing here. I must be crazy."

Or they'll say, "You notice the old people on the reservation. They got all the secrets. They know a lot of things Indians in town don't know . . . ."

"Like what?" the town children ask.

"Indian things. Secrets."

Maybe it's true. Maria remembers some of those secrets—the power in eagle feathers and in songs and dreams and dances and stones, the power in animals. Desert animals know so much more than poor stupid people about how to live on the earth. Horned toads and deer and coyotes and mountain lions. Snakes. Spiders. They have lived here longer than people.

Maria brushes her hair, ties a scarf over her head, and looks around for her shoes—frayed tennis shoes from St. Vincent de Paul secondhand store.

She has been working for Mrs. Quincy for two or three years now, one day a week if she can make it. Mrs. Quincy always asks her, "How's the family?" and Maria answers, "Okay."

Today it's the same thing. "Okay. Fine," Maria says. She's never told her that Joe Vasquez left a long time ago or that they don't have a house right now. And when she doesn't turn up for work for a week or two she never tells Mrs. Quincy why. Or if she does say anything it's just, "One of the kids was sick . . . ." or "I went to the reservation." Never the truth. Never the hangover or the ten days in jail or the fact that you don't have a dime for a phone call or a quarter for the bus. Never the feeling that, Holy Mother, how can I make it over there this morning . . . .

Today as she scrubs floors and waxes and washes windows and irons white shirts Maria keeps glancing toward the mountains where clouds are beginning to gather. That doesn't mean rain yet. Maybe not today at all. Maybe tomorrow. And if it should come today she knows her children will run to the abandoned car there in the alley. Still, it doesn't have glass in the windows.

When she's through work Maria has seven dollars and some change and a pair of Mrs. Quincy's old shoes in a paper sack.

By the time she gets off the southside bus there is the faint faraway sound of thunder. How many months has it been? People around the street corner in front of the B-29 bar are all looking up toward the sky too. Who doesn't have a roof that leaks somewhere? Who doesn't have a window or two without glass? Who doesn't have mattresses outside the house where the nights are cooler? And yet the town Papagos still feel a strange distant excitement at the thought of those first summer rains. You can see that the Indians have a secret look about them when the rains come, for even if they missed the sahuaro fruit picking and took no part at all in preparing wine, for the summer rainmaking feast they are still touched by it. It's still for them. And who has been away from home so long he doesn't feel a surge of well-being when the first drops splat against the dry burning earth.

Errol Flynn and Anna and Amelia are waiting at the bus stop for Maria. Maria knows why, and nobody has to say it but Amelia says it anyway. "Give us the money, Mama, before you get beer. Somebody might steal it or you might get drunk and lose it."

Maria hands the money to Anna. "I'll just keep one quarter. You go to the store and then put what's left in that tin can."

"Okay, Mama."

"I won't stay long. Just until dark."

The children go down the street toward the Chinese market and Maria opens the door of the B-29. As soon as she goes in, the dimness enfolds her and she stands there by the door until she can see. No hurrying now that she's here where she has been headed all day.

Rose lifts her head toward Maria and Maria goes to the table where Rose and Lopez sit together on a wooden bench. There's a man on the other side, another Papago. Maria used to know him she thinks, maybe when they were kids at Phoenix Indian school. Before either of them were fat. Nothing yet to show whether he is the one she dreamed of ... whether he laughs sometimes or whether he is always silent, whether he will take her to the reservation for feast days, whether he will hit her when he drinks.

All four give a greeting in Papago.

"Rain yet?" Rose asks.

Maria shakes her head. "Maybe tonight."

"They better get a roof over that swimming pool before the rain comes. We might have to swim in it yet," Lopez says. He nods toward his cousin across the table, says to Maria, "This guy's been helping me all day. We been to the dump getting good stuff to make the roof. Some real good tin, good boards too."

They pour a glass of beer for Maria. She brings out her twenty-five cents but the man beside her — she still doesn't know his name — pushes it back to her. So she knows that the dream was true and this is the man.

No sign from her, of course. She doesn't even glance toward him.

She's glad he's fat. She'd hate to go to bed with a skinny man, hate to feel a man's ribs or shoulder blades or thigh bones. A man should have a belly round as a hill. And there should be enough of him so a woman can feel warm and safe against him. You want to know he won't blow away with the first little wind that comes across the desert. Then if the woman is soft and plump and round herself they can roll easy as foxes in the sand. Oh, they can roll . . . .

After a long time, Lopez tells Maria, "This guy, my cousin, Manny, is the smart one. He's a detective."

Maria hopes it's a joke. That doesn't sound like an Indian job.

But Manny nods. "That's right. I'm studying for that kind of work."

"Detective school?"

"It's mail order," he says. "I got the book. I study every night . . . send in papers and everything."

Maria is shaken. Fate could send her any man — a man who drank and didn't work at all, maybe a man who did a little building or picked melons or chopped cotton. But she hadn't expected a man from detective school. Well, he'll sure catch me if I do anything wrong . . . .

"I pay four dollars a week for the lessons," he says. "Ace Training School. Parker, Ohio."

"He could keep us all out of jail," Rose says. "If we were arrested."

Manny shrugs but they all look at him, impressed.

They have four more glasses of beer each. From time to time when someone opens the door they all look toward the darkness, but somebody who is closer always says, "No rain. Not yet." So they settle back and talk and Maria feels Manny's leg against her.

Finally he says to her, "Listen, you got a desk at your place? I need a desk to sit at to do my detective lesson."

Maria looks down embarrassed, but Rose laughs. "No desk! Man, she got no house!"

Manny shrugs. "Just an orange crate or something would do, I guess."

"I got cardboard boxes, that's all."

"That might do," he says. "Sure, that would be fine."

"How come a desk anyway?" Lopez asks.

Manny reaches down on the bench beside him and brings up the loose-leaf folder of Ace lessons, opens it to Lesson III. Reads aloud: "Always sit at your desk to prepare your lessons. Be sure your desk is neat. Papers should be carefully stacked. Pencils should be sharpened. Your finger nails should be clean, your clothes neat. Remember, you are a detective!"

Maria knows now how important this man is. As important as a social worker. Important as the man who books you into county jail. The loan company man. The judge. Schoolteachers. That's the kind of people who have desks. And of course detectives too.

Maria doesn't know him well enough yet to ask questions, but Rose can ask: "Listen, what did you do for a desk before? Did you have one?"

"I just done two lessons over at Yuma while I was picking oranges. I sat down on the ground. But I checked off the place where the paper said 'Is your desk neat?'"

"How'd you check it?" Lopez asks. "Yes or no?"

"Man, I checked it 'YES'."

"Well, if they're such smart detectives how come they don't know you're lying?"

Manny shrugs. "I bet they would of thrown me out of the school if they knew I didn't have that desk."

"Sure," Rose says. "A detective's supposed to have one."

You can see he's smart in white man's ways as well as Indian ways. If he can fool a detective school maybe he'd be able to fool a social worker too. He'd know what to say to them.

Maria is a little drunk now, happy and warm, and her arms and legs feel as loose as leaves on a mesquite branch. She knows that this whole month has been a time of great good fortune in the neighborhood with St. Jude handing out that swimming pool to Elma Domingo. So now it might be Jude himself sending this smart Papago detective to solve her own problems. Of course Maria hadn't asked Jude for a man. When she passed by the shrine yesterday she didn't even light a candle, though she nodded her head and thought, look, I could do with some flour and some lard. And a house too. But she would never have asked for a man. Let Jude help with something really hard—like a house. You can't ask a saint for everything. You got to do something for yourself.

The truth is Maria has never done much for Jude and he's never done much for her. Until now. But you can see that this is no ordinary man, this fine fat smart detective.

Maria lifts her glass. Makes a silent vow to Jude, good old wise friend Jude.

"Where you living?" Manny asks Maria as he rolls a cigarette.

"Outdoors," she says. "Across the alley by Domingo's, just across from the swimming pool."

"I got to stay there and help them with the roof for that thing," Manny says. "I figured I sleep there."

"It sure is nice sleeping by the pool," Lopez says.

"It's a real pretty place," Rose says. "Even without water."

Manny turns to Maria. "We could go sit in the car there. You know that old car."

"Sure," Maria says. "If somebody's not already there."

Of course they know that someone is probably in the car. This time of night it will either be lovers clinging together in the back seat or some poor wino who's been locked out of his own family's house and falls asleep in the front seat with the door open and his feet dangling out. Maybe kids smoking marijuana and laughing. Even the stray dogs know about that car.

In this part of town a car, whether it runs or not, is to be admired. You'll see one parked in front of somebody's house for months at a time, maybe years, waiting for a new motor, battery, tires. Girls come and sit in it in the evenings and boys lean against it casually as they smoke, as they pass around the bottle of wine, as they tell jokes. Even the old car in the alley still has its bit of fringe hanging from the back window and a saint on the dashboard and a new **VOTE FOR RAMIREZ** sticker on the bumper.

When Maria and Manny get to the car they hesitate but there's no sound at all. Finally Manny goes up close and peers in. He opens the door gently — "With your permission, Mr. Flores. You better go on home now" — hauls out the sleeping wino, the empty bottle still in his hand. The old man stands there for a minute unable to focus his eyes, but Manny puts his straw hat on his head and turns him in the direction of the Friendship Mission. Then Manny opens the car door for Maria and she steps in, sinks back, comfortable, dizzy, vaguely aware of the far-off smell of coming rain. Rain somewhere back in the mountains. Rain somewhere sending the scent of greasewood bushes cutting through the hot dry desert air.

A car is all right, but Maria wishes they were on the ground. Their large plump bodies are cramped in the back seat. They need space and air and earth . . . hillsides, arroyos, valleys, sand.

"You know that park down the street?" she says.

"I know it." They get out of the car and start walking. Maria has left her shoes in the car but it doesn't matter. She has never liked to feel shoes on her feet. Anyway there is grass at the park and it is soft and cool.

This is a small park, more like a plaza in a Mexican village. Just a few benches and a small fountain that doesn't work anymore. Iris. Oleander. Curved walks. A few pink petunias. Marijuana growing among the trumpet vines in the cement planters.

It's so late now that the park is empty and the lights are off except for the one at the street corner. Manny puts his Ace Training School notebook on the bench and they lie under the dark, bending oleanders. Maria almost wishes she hadn't had so much beer because she's afraid she won't remember tomorrow how good it felt to have a man again. She's afraid she'll forget some moment of it, some of the soft moaning pleasure.

But suddenly the sprinklers come on. Manny yells out. He's on top of her so he feels it first. He rolls off and covers his face with his arms. The next curve of water hits Maria and she rolls over on her stomach and lies there with her face in the grass cursing gently.

Manny grabs his shoes and pulls on his pants and Maria runs heavily beside him through the high arches of spray to the cement walk. They sit on the bench wiping water off their faces.

"Be careful you don't drip on my detective papers," Manny says.

"Not me."

After awhile they walk back down the alley but this time they see a man and a woman getting into the car.

"Hell," Manny says. "We sure got bad luck."

"It's okay," Maria says. "You come to my bed." So they walk on past the car down the dark dusty alley to the back yard where Maria's cardboard boxes are scattered and her children are sleeping.

Errol Flynn has rolled out of bed and is curled up on the ground. Maria lifts the baby onto the mattress with Anna and Amelia, and then she comes back to Manny and touches him, and thinks, so this is where Jude wanted him after all. In my own bed.

If you have a man in your bed what else do you need?

Manny finds a place on the ground for his Ace detective notebook, covers it with his shirt and pants. See how he folds them. Maria knows how her own would be in a heap however they fell.

Just at the moment that he puts his heavy round body next to Maria's they feel the first slow sweet drop of summer rain. Not hard rain. Not carried on the wind. It's light and tender and each separate drop comes alone, taking its time, easy and gentle. It lasts only a few minutes, more like the memory of rain than rain itself. The children don't even wake, don't know they've been rained on, but Manny and Maria pull the torn piece of sheet over their heads as though they were being drenched, put their arms around each other and begin to laugh.

People who are used to being crowded together, a whole family in a room, learn to keep their lovemaking quiet as animals in a burrow, quiet as a hill of grass moving in the wind. And children learn that the night is full of adult sounds that may be crying, may be laughing. Somebody dreaming, whispering secrets. The children always listen but they can't be sure; it's just a part of their sleep.

Sometime toward morning there is another drop or so, still not much, not enough to make corn grow. "Maybe you better get you a house," Manny says.

Maria nods her head against him. "I can't until I get the welfare money. And I can't get the welfare money until I get me an address. That's their rule. Maybe they need to know where to send the money."

Manny must know about rules. He's probably read the whole book of them. He'll know what to do.

"They say you need a house number, no?"

She nods, rubs her hand along his face. "It sure would be a lot easier if I had the money first."

He sits up in bed. "I think I got it, all right. We'll go ask Elma Domingo can you use her house number."

Maria doesn't understand at first. "They got so many people there already."

"No," he says. "All you need to borrow is the number on the mailbox—not the house. Just the address, see. But over at welfare they'll think you got the house too."

"That's right. How would they know?"

They lie down again. "You could even put some of your boxes and maybe your cook stove over there. Then if welfare came around, they'd see your stuff there."

See. It's so easy after all. You have to know how to look at white people's rules. You can't expect them to make sense in the Indian way. Maybe when *I'itoi* brought the people up from the underworld and showed them his ways of planting and hunting and curing illnesses and bringing rain and keeping harmony—even how to make sahuaro wine for the rainmaking feast—he should have also told them how to understand white people's rules.

"It's your detective training made you figure out what to do," Maria says.

"Yeah, I guess it is."

She doesn't tell him, of course, that Jude sent him here to her, put him into her bed just so these problems would be solved. All she says is, "I'm going to make you tortillas as soon as it's light enough to see."

But they go to sleep and the sun is up when they wake. Jane and Amelia and Carmen are sitting on the bed with them looking at Manny. It takes him a few minutes to open his eyes.

"Hi," the children say.

Manny nods to them.

"Listen," Amelia says, "did you find us a house last night, Mama?"

"Not really that," Maria says. "But I think maybe we found us an address. A number at least . . . ."

"I rather have a house," Amelia insists.

"Me too," says Jane.

"That comes next," Maria says, still not even sitting up. "First the address."

CHAPTER 7

LUPE SERRA

This is one of Lupe's bad times. The spirits in her body fight over her. The terrible forces of magic pull at her insides until she can feel herself being stretched apart — liver, heart, arms, legs, intestines. Her belly almost rips open. Her eyes push outward. Her mind is jagged around the edges, sharp as a broken wine bottle. And she feels blood moving inside her, sloshing like waves against her bones.

She just looks at them when they try to persuade her to stir the frijoles or sweep the yard or follow the baby around.

When it takes all your strength to keep your own poor thin body from breaking open, what else can you do? How can you wash a tub of clothes? How can you go chasing after children? The only hope is to lie down and hold on to something, the edge of the mattress, anything. Stay close to the ground. Try to make the sign of the cross once in a while. Drink a tea of *ruda* or rub your breasts and neck with special ashes that old people keep in a cloth bag. Try certain herbs and weeds that people bring from the mountains.

Now she squats in the dirt under the palo verde tree watching the people who come every evening to peer into the huge blue cement hole that is Mrs. Domingo's swimming pool. Lupe herself won't go near it. She only watches from under the tree.

"It's nothing to fear. Just a hole in the earth. Just that," Mrs. Domingo tells her daughter.

But Lupe shudders. A hole in the earth is a grave. Why else would these men with their great digging machines have come and ripped up the rocks and weeds and even the woodpile.

"A grave," Lupe whispers. "A blue grave."

Every day she puts on her black dress for mourning and sometimes she wraps a black mantilla around her head too.

"It sure takes the fun out of it. Really it does," Ignacio admits.

They have pulled a bench up to the edge of the pool and the women sit on that. The men stand around the little heap of boards and tin that they have donated to help make a roof for the swimming pool.

The Ramada Builder has been down in the pool all afternoon, stepping off the distance here and there, looking first at his feet, then up to the sky, frowning and chuckling and talking quietly to himself as he scratches his head. This is no easy job like roofing a ramada. Here you have to think of the slope. You have to consider, too, that there never was a mesquite tree tall enough or straight enough to make the kind of post you need.

Lupe hears them talking but she never can be certain anymore which voices are the ones in her head and which ones come from other people.

Nobody forgets Lupe. Every few minutes someone — Lopez or Rose or even the children — glances over toward her. Now Rose goes to her and says, "If you'd come look in you'd see how it's all plastered so pretty and the steps go part way down and it's all blue around the edge."

Maria's oldest girl, Anna, has followed Rose. She tells Lupe, "They don't make graves that way."

"Sometimes they do. Now and then they do."

"Not with a railing by the steps."

"Maybe white people do," Lupe whispers, and now Anna looks doubtful too.

Of course Lupe has never looked into a swimming pool before, one with or without water. This isn't the swimming pool part of town. Here you just take off your shoes and wade in the street when the July rains come down.

Lupe takes a few steps toward the pool. She can hear the children playing in it running and sliding, jumping from the step to the bottom, but she doesn't want her own children there. What if the priest came and said his prayers and threw dirt over them and buried them in there.

"No, no," she screams to the baby, Josefina. So the women sitting on the bench carry Josefina back to her.

There is a certain respect here for one touched by Spirits or Beings or witchcraft. Everyone knows these sleepless tormented ones hold within themselves a knowledge no one else has. They remember fears and mysteries the others have forgotten. They see clearly the slow dark shapes that are hidden from others. When they hear an owl cry at night they know the terror others have lost the name for.

Lupe holds her child and lies down on the mattress again but her eyes are open wide.

Lupe's illness began two years ago when she and Ignacio and the baby Josefina — not yet baptized — were living over to the west of town near the cotton fields. Ignacio worked in the fields then hoeing cotton. Lupe was like anybody else. She made good thin tortillas every morning before sunup so Ignacio would have them fresh and soft for lunch, wrapped around frijoles and chilles. She cooked beans then too and swept the dirt floor of their house every day and sprinkled it with a little water. She laughed and danced and drank tequila with Ignacio on Saturday nights when he got paid, and she curled her hair then too. Like anybody else.

But it was her bad luck that a *bruja,* a witch, lived in the shack next to theirs. They say her powers were so great that she could make Ignacio leave Lupe's bed at night and come to hers instead. Her magic was so strong that even though he wanted to go home, his legs had no strength and he could never make it to the door and had to stay with her all night. She clouded his sight so that he believed this witch was beautiful though half her teeth were gone and she was ten years older than Lupe and skinny as a jack rabbit. They say the saints in her house were turned to the wall and that she had a book written in Spanish which told how to put spells on those you wished to get rid of.

It was Lupe's bad luck that this woman had to have Ignacio. This is how it happened: the woman came to the door of her shack and yelled out, "Come on and have some coffee before you start the wash. Come on and have some little cakes."

And Lupe had left Josefina sleeping by a greasewood bush and run over to the woman's place. Lupe was hungry because the witchcraft caused her to yearn for any kind of little cake, anything sweet.

They didn't go into the house. The woman brought two tin cups out under the ramada and they sat down on some large flat rocks there in the shade, and sure enough there was a thick yellow cake in the pan. Of course a *bruja* likes to use a certain white powder to do her magic when it is a man she wants, so she had put that powder in Lupe's coffee. One taste and Lupe knew it. One taste and she felt her bones going soft. She threw that coffee to the ground and ran, but the evil was a grey *reboza*, a shawl, around her and it stayed with her. People who saw her running across the desert that day remember seeing it. They all speak of that *reboza.*

Other women heard her screams and hurried outside, but there are only a few shacks at this place and no one knew just what to do for her. Even Ignacio heard her from the field and he left his hoe and went to find her, but by that time she had run to the priest and fallen at his feet clasping his ankles and begging for his blessing.

"Father, take this spell off me. Do it or I'll die!"

"Stand up. Get yourself up."

But she couldn't move and she lay there in the dirt crying and pleading and hiding her eyes from the sun.

"A blessing . . . just a blessing . . . ." They said that's what she kept begging for. Then she tried to push open the door of the church but he held it.

"You can't go bellowing and slobbering into God's house," he said. "You can't act like a heathen here."

She kept trying to get in anyway. She even hit her head against the door, but the priest wouldn't let her in. Finally the other women came and pulled her away and somebody put a rosary in her hand but the priest went into the church and locked the door and didn't come out all afternoon.

Lupe can still remember all that. Other things cloud in her mind, lie in a junk yard of memories, bent beyond recognition, but not that day. That day is clear. That sun never fades. She still tastes that white powder. A hundred times she has tried to wash her mouth clean. She's even scraped her teeth with branches of *yerba colorado* gathered along the washes on the reservation, but nothing works. Rainwater doesn't work. Neither does white arroyo sand. Of course, nobody really expects her to be cured so easily. She doesn't expect it either. When a spell is strong you need a stronger one to work against it.

The Papago medicine man, the *maka:ii* from near Baboquivari Mountain is said to be good at this kind of thing. He knows ways of sucking out whatever object the witch has shot into one's body . . . sharp stone or pin or ant or spider or even a wad of dry mud.

Or perhaps the *curandero* who comes up from Sonora might help. He has special herbs and smokes magic cigarettes which he gets from the Yaquis.

"If they give me anything over at welfare, then you can count on me for a couple of dollars," Maria says. And Lopez tells them, "I got a job for next week. Sure." And even the Ramada Builder, the loco one, looks in his pocket when he hears them talking but all he finds is a little blue rock and a penny.

So they do what they can in the meantime by boiling certain roots and lighting candles over at St. Jude, but you don't expect success.

"If the *bruja* would just repent," Mrs. Domingo says, time after time.

"Or if we had a stronger power to put against her," old Mrs. Reyes murmurs.

But Lupe has no power at all. She feels that lack of power more than she feels anything else. When you've been witched your whole body seems to move outside the mind. Weightless, limp, pushed and pulled by any wind, by an owl cry, by any fear—fear has its own shape now—or by the morning air as it moves across the vacant lots. You can be lifted up by the voices in your head. You can be forced down flat to the ground by the shadow of a bird. The movement of leaves in a tree can pull a scream up out of your dry throat.

Everyone around, everyone who knows, feels himself somehow affected by the great power acting on Lupe. "We'll gather up that money one of these days," they say. But who really has the hope of an extra five dollars this month?

Ignacio can't help. He has no job now. Would a *bruja* who has any power at all be foolish enough to let the husband of the witched woman make enough money to pay a medicine man? Would she go to so much trouble to get a man for herself and then give up so easily? Not her. So no one expects Ignacio to find a job. He watches the children and he watches Lupe too when Mrs. Domingo goes to do housework for somebody. And sometimes his friends, knowing his sadness and his bad luck, bring over a bottle of tokay and sit with him under the mesquite tree through an afternoon. They push their straw hats back on their heads and play a guitar and sing and talk.

Lupe lies across the yard under the palo verde tree listening to them, hearing strange messages in what they say, hidden sounds that follow behind spoken words. Women come to visit her, old ones and young ones too, everyone knowing that this thing could happen to any one of them. When someone like that *bruja* with her book of magic decides to go after a man, she doesn't have to say a thing. She doesn't have to laugh or flick her eyes or curl her hair or unbutton her blouse or run her hand along his neck or cook for him. All she has to do is leave her door unlocked. He'll be there as soon as the sun goes down. And is it his fault, poor fellow?

Lupe sleeps a little during the day, maybe five or ten minutes at a time, wakes with a bad taste of white powder in her mouth, has to have water.

The time she can't sleep at all is nighttime. At night she walks wherever it is dark. Restless, she slips through alleys, barefooted, long black hair hanging wild around her shoulders. Tonight she's changed from the black dress and she's wearing a man's grey terrycloth bathrobe they found in a box of give-away clothes from one of the white ladies Rose sometimes works for. The robe is so large it's wrapped around her almost twice and the sleeves hang down past her fingers. Under it she's naked.

The only other person awake this late is the Ramada Builder. Lupe sees him sitting there beside the great hole in the earth, the deep grave or swimming pool or whatever it is. He's looking down into it, and he mumbles to himself and shakes his head and scratches his thick black hair. But he looks up as Lupe goes by and calls out to her, "Look what I got to do."

"What?" she says, but she won't go closer.

"I got to put a roof on this big house. Me. I got to do it."

"Okay," she says.

"Listen," he says. "You can't dig no post holes in that hard cement. And that's the way you got to make a ramada; you got to dig post holes." He climbs up from the edge of the pool and is ready to walk with her but she doesn't want to hear any more talk that she can't understand so she turns and runs down the alley.

His voice comes after her, still puzzled. "We sure got to find a tall mesquite somewhere . . . ."

Across the alley is the house where Maria Vasquez and her children are sleeping out in the back yard. She passes the abandoned car which sits flat down in the dirt of the alley and she hears the long rhythmical moans and gasps of a man and woman coming up from the depths of the back seat. She pauses, listening for a second or two, moves on toward the B-29 bar where both the sour fumes of yellow beer and the loud crying music seep through the adobe walls.

But she turns back toward the alleys. Doesn't want people to stop her. Doesn't want men to make her lie down with them in the shadows behind some bush. Doesn't want a police car to put its light on her. Doesn't want anybody . . . anybody . . . to talk to her. Wants to find a place where strength can come up to her out of the earth. Goes down by the railroad tracks, up past the freeway. But she can't find a good place.

Now she is afraid to sleep, afraid that terrible things will happen if she lets her eyes close. She gets tired walking and squats down where she is, just a vacant lot, anywhere, no special place.

A dog comes by, licks her legs, but she doesn't move. That dog could be anything . . . a witch. She doesn't look at it.

There are always people moving around at night. Lupe doesn't mind seeing Indians. They won't hurt her. It's the white people she knows she'd better stay away from.

Indians recognize bad luck when they see it and they'll do what they can for you. But if white people notice you've got a spell on you they'll lock you up in their hospital and then you never have a chance to get well because you can't get the herbs and medicines that might help you. You can't ever see a medicine man.

Lupe doesn't want to stop walking. Sometimes she has to lie down wherever she falls to catch her breath before she can go on again.

She's flat on her back in the vacant lot across from the Ave Maria garage when she becomes aware that the Ramada Builder is trying to drag something up the curb.

These two are both used to the dark. They see in it. They move through it easier than they do daylight. Like coyotes. Like owls.

The Ramada Builder isn't surprised to see Lupe lying there among the weeds and rocks and broken glass. He nods and tries to wave but what he is pulling is too heavy. Finally he lets it down and comes over to her. He just points to it.

Lupe lifts her head, sees that it is a telephone pole.

"Too heavy," the Ramada Builder says, shaking his head. "Too heavy."

Lupe isn't surprised to find the Ramada Builder there struggling with a telephone pole in the middle of the night. She doesn't ask him anything, just looks at it.

"But I sure like it," the Ramada Builder says. "I like it a lot. I like how straight she grows."

It is straight. Lupe sees that.

"Tall too," the Ramada Builder says. "It sure is good and tall."

Lupe leans forward to get a better look but she doesn't rise.

The Ramada Builder is proud. "You help me a little bit," he pleads. "Maybe we get it home. Us two." His big uneven face lights up just thinking about it.

Lupe can't smile with him. Even so, she gets up and pulls the stickers out of her feet and they go to the curb and begin to roll the thing up over the cement and across the vacant lot. Around the corner is St. Jude. They stop and rest here, both breathing heavily.

Lupe doesn't ask why they are taking the telephone pole. But a couple of winos who have just left the B-29 bar come up beside them and stand gazing down at the Ramada Builder's prize.

"How come you stealing that?"

The Ramada Builder says, "Me?" He sounds surprised — so honestly surprised that even the winos know it's just something he found. Just his good luck.

"Man, you sure got you a good telephone pole there."

"It was just laying there. Wasn't nobody using it."

Then the Ramada Builder remembers that there was another one with it that he wanted to go back for. "Come on. Maybe you help me get that other one."

So Lupe and the two winos and the Ramada Builder leave one pole at the shrine of St. Jude and go after the other one. It's there on a corner where a new school is being built, but even with a street light on they don't have any trouble. The two winos aren't able to stand very straight but the pole itself helps to balance them as they move along.

It takes an hour, maybe less, to drag both poles up to the edge of the pool. Of course there's a good bit of talking and singing by the winos now and maybe a little noise in banging the poles against the abandoned car as they come down the alley, and there are a few dogs following along and barking.

Ignacio wakes and comes outside. So does Mrs. Domingo, her long hair in braids that hang to her waist. Rose and Lopez come out of the abandoned car. And Maria's boy, Errol Flynn, slips away from the yard where he's been sleeping on the ground. They all gather around the telephone poles, stand there stretching and yawning from time to time, just looking . . . admiring.

"We ought to get them covered up before morning," Lopez says. "Somebody might want them back."

Mrs. Domingo nods. "See. Jude even gave us a little moonlight. Not full, of course, but a little."

Everybody lines up and they roll one of the telephone poles over the curb, lift it off the ground and place it lengthwise across the pool. Then the other. The poles extend at least two feet on each edge. Perfect. God be praised. The Ramada Builder pats the edge of the wood tenderly with his big rough hands and everyone stands there looking pleased and surprised. Here you don't really expect success; it comes as a surprise — when it comes.

Lupe isn't part of the group. She has backed away and stands in the shadows moaning softly as the rest of them work. She can't understand why they're going to so much work to cover a grave. Of course she knows that Papagos always do what they can to make graves pretty. Pink and blue crosses. Paper flowers. Ribbons. Candles. Presents for the dead. But here she sees them piling up bits of lumber, two-by-fours, pieces of plywood still bearing the photograph of some political candidate, wide strips of frayed canvas and sheet metal from the city dump. All of this goes over the telephone poles, completely covers them.

By morning all you can see is the junk heap that roofs over the pool, hides the telephone poles. Lupe watches, thinking only that she likes paper flowers better for a grave.

CHAPTER 8

MRS. DOMINGO

Since this Manny Escalante figured out the way to get an address for Maria to give to the welfare lady, word has spread that he has the knack of understanding how Anglos think. Mrs. Domingo admires this talent, and she likes to question him. She herself enjoys discovering hidden meanings, omens, signs. She's wise, but wise in Indian ways, not Anglo ways.

Indians know that a white person will choose whatever makes the most trouble for everyone; he'll never think of the natural easy way that would come first to an Indian's mind. So it's not just anyone who can ever guess how those minds are working, what strange paths they follow.

Today Mrs. Domingo is sitting in a rocking chair down in the deep end of the swimming pool. Rose and Lopez are stretched out on the slanting cement floor asleep, their heavy shoes touching. Manny and Maria are in the two straight chairs facing Mrs. Domingo, watching as she rolls a Bull Durham cigarette. She'd never smoke out in the sunlight, but now that she's old she can take that kind of pleasure in private among her friends.

It's dark down here, secret and magical with just the flickering light of the candles grouped around the pictures of St. Jude and St. Francis Xavier and the Virgin of Guadalupe.

They've moved a few of Maria's cardboard boxes down into the swimming pool, and the pictures of the saints are propped up on them. If anybody from welfare comes around, Maria knows what she is supposed to say: "See, that's my stuff. I live right here."

She's practiced saying it to Manny. A whisper. She can't bring her voice up out of her throat when she thinks of speaking to a social worker, but Manny tells her, "You got to speak out the way *they* do. They'll never believe you unless you talk loud."

Now Manny is leaning forward explaining again how the idea of the address came into his mind. It's something you can discuss many times.

"That's just one of the regular rules over there at welfare," he says. "No rent money to be given out to anybody who hasn't got a house."

"Seems to me they'd give you the money quicker than ever if they knew you didn't have a roof over your head." She draws on her cigarette, holding it carefully between her thumb and forefinger.

"Not them," Manny says. "They got a whole different way of seeing things."

Mrs. Domingo considers it from another angle. "What if she'd said she had a house all right but there just wasn't a number on it anywhere? I've seen houses like that."

"That wouldn't help," he says. "If their rule says they want a number, then you got to get one for them. Never mind the house. Just so you got the number. They really stick to things like that."

"They do," Maria nods.

They sit awhile in silence, hearing the slow steady whine of Lopez' breathing and the voices of the children above ground, outside. But all three of them suddenly tense and Manny stands up. The children's voices have changed. You catch the tight careful sound that moves into Indian voices when an Anglo is present.

"It could be somebody to see you," Mrs. Domingo whispers to Maria. "Remember, you just act like this is your place right here. Don't even look over at the alley."

Maria nods.

They can't quite hear what the children are saying, but there's no doubt they aren't talking to an Indian. You can tell that.

In this part of town even the youngest children know about answering questions and opening doors. You learn to peek out first. Just the slightest flutter of the curtains, the faintest whisper behind the door. If it's a white face, you wait for it to go away. Five. Ten. Fifteen minutes. White people don't like to wait long. But if they do wait and you finally open the door an inch, you pretend not to speak English. Or if you do speak English, you say (even if it's your brother they're asking for), "No, I wouldn't know that name. I never heard of that one around here. No. I don't know."

Mrs. Domingo gets up stiffly, hands her cigarette to Manny. "I'm the one to find out," she says.

The floor of the pool slants so it's like climbing a steep little hill. The blue steps don't reach all the way to the floor, and there is an old bucket below the steps to climb onto first. It takes awhile.

As you come up you have to stoop to keep from hitting your head against the telephone poles and corrugated tin **Pepsi Cola** sign and cardboard that make the roof. You fold yourself over like any desert creature coming out of his burrow. Small as a gopher, you reach up toward sunlight. It is good to go from darkness to light; it recalls those first Papagos who struggled upward from the underworld.

But Mrs. Domingo has to wait a moment more to reach the light because the entrance to the pool now has a little shack built over it to keep the rain out. From the street it looks like any outhouse rising unsteadily from any pile of junk.

Mrs. Domingo peers out through the holes in this door before she pushes it open.

At first she can't even guess that the girl standing there in the sun talking to the children might be a social worker. They're so skinny and small, these white girls, how can you tell whether they're children or women? They dress like children anyway. Look at this one . . . bare suntanned legs, sandals, short red dress way above her knees, long blonde hair swinging loose. An Indian has sense enough to know when she changes from girl to woman. Not these Anglos. They don't know the pleasures of the many seasons of life, don't know the satisfaction of ripening.

The girl has a puzzled look on her face. She is smiling at the children and now she turns quickly to smile at Mrs. Domingo too. But Mrs. Domingo is old enough that she doesn't have to smile for nothing the way white women do whether they mean it or not. So she waits. Just stands there.

This girl has an armful of papers. "I'm Sue Mills . . . from the welfare department."

The children move back and look at her, expectant, as though she might play a game with them. Even so, they're wary.

She's still smiling toward the children, first one and then another. Seven of them.

"They don't all live here, do they?"

"Them?" Mrs. Domingo glances around the yard as though she had never before noticed these shabby barefoot ones. Her grandchildren. She peers into their round dark faces.

Three of them are Rose's kids. Four are Lupe's. Lupe's little ones are still so young they can't understand that their mother has been taken away and they have looked for her all day behind trees, in abandoned cars, in the ruins of the unfinished adobe house. Poor Lupe, locked up now in that hospital where Anglos put crazy people. If only they had waited until the medicine man had a chance to cure her . . . but Lupe had gone running through the streets at night. Of course they found her. And now nobody knows when she'll be home again.

"Mrs. Domingo?"

"Yes."

"I really have to ask. How many children are living here with you?"

Mrs. Domingo shrugs. "These kids from down the street? But they're just hanging around. That's all." She waves her arms, shouts at them in Papago, again roughly in English. "Go on home, you kids. Beat it."

And they go, bare feet kicking up dust as they streak across the vacant lot. Mrs. Domingo knows they'll run around the corner and wait until the white girl has gone. They all have sense enough for that. Even the three-year-old, Josefina. She is right behind the others, not looking back.

But this Sue Mills says in her excited little-girl voice, "The thing is, Mrs. Domingo, we've already had a complaint from the health department."

Mrs. Domingo sits down slowly on a log in the woodpile. "I got a few complaints myself," she says. She won't let them frighten her the way the younger women are always frightened.

Still smiling (Holy Mother, doesn't she ever stop that!) Sue Mills flings back her hair and sits down beside Mrs. Domingo, crossing her long suntanned legs in the sand. She hands two papers to Mrs. Domingo — one yellow, one white. But Mrs. Domingo doesn't even glance down at them. She waits for the girl to tell her.

"Inadequate plumbing . . . lack of running water . . . improper . . . ."

"But we got an outhouse," Mrs. Domingo says.

"Yes, I see you have two of them." She smiles enthusiastically.

But Mrs. Domingo corrects her. "Only one. Why would we want two?"

Sue Mills glances toward the privy behind the two-room tin shack, then toward the thin little building huddled at the entrance of the swimming pool.

"Oh, that," Mrs. Domingo says. "That's to the swimming pool."

The girl jumps up and starts toward it, hesitates when she notices that the earth around it is covered with layers of tin and boards and palm fronds. Tacked to the door is a Virgin of Guadalupe poster which says **THIS IS A CATHOLIC HOUSE.** Someone has crossed out the word, **HOUSE,** and pencilled above it, **SWIM POOL.**

Mrs. Domingo watches the young social worker standing there in the sun squinting at the rough splintery boards of that doorway. But she does not make any explanation and the girl doesn't turn around for a long time. When she does, all she says is, "Wow!"

Mrs. Domingo usually brings out a chair when any important person comes to the house but this afternoon she doesn't because the two straight chairs and the rocking chair are all down in the swimming pool. Anyway, this girl is so young . . . and she doesn't stay anywhere for very long.

They sit down on pieces of mesquite in the woodpile and Sue Mills chews on her large pink sunglasses as she talks. "I really hate to bring bad news," she says. "But the health department says the house has been known to be substandard for a long time and when you wash there's water running in the alley and . . . ." She studies the papers. "And in a substandard two-room house, you cannot take in other people's children."

Mrs. Domingo relaxes, feels the muscles of her neck loosen. "It's okay then. I don't want to take in other people's children. To tell the truth, I never thought of it. I got enough trouble feeding my own grandkids."

The girl begins to shake her head even before she says anything. "But that's what they're talking about. Grandchildren."

"*Them?*"

"Now that your daughter . . . ." She studies the yellow paper for the name. "Now that Lupe has been committed to the state hospital her children are eligible to be placed in foster homes and taken care of."

Mrs. Domingo doesn't speak yet. Just looks at the girl, looks at the sky, looks at the brown earth.

"Then, of course, the welfare department would pay for their care."

After a while Mrs. Domingo says, "Well, if welfare wants to pay somebody, let welfare pay me for their food. Two or three dollars now and then. That would do."

Sue Mills leans forward, her blue eyes round and bright. "Oh, a *relative* can't be certified as a foster parent."

Mrs. Domingo's face is blank, expressionless. She is glad to feel the sun on her, hot as it is; that's something she can understand.

"It's a rule, you know," the girl says finally.

"Who made that rule?" But she asks it quietly under her breath. Who thought of that one? Surely not an Indian. There's not an Indian in Arizona dumb enough to make a rule like that.

Mrs. Domingo thinks of the round one-room house where she was born out there on the reservation, a place made of bent ocotillo sticks covered with bunches of grass. A family in a room together ... what's bad about that? It is a very good thing for a family to come together into its own small circle of light. It is a very good thing to hear each other's nighttime breathing. And who stays in a house so much anyway—except white people. An Indian is outside most of the time.

"Tell them we don't need that money," Mrs. Domingo says.

The girl looks distressed. Her smile is gone. "Really, I know how you feel. But the health department seems to think that . . . ."

The papers lie between them on the ground. They both glance toward them. The girl seems lost in thought now but Mrs. Domingo knows something must be done, so she pulls herself up and leads the way over to the tin shack.

"Look here," she says, poking at a cardboard patch in the wall with the mesquite stick she is leaning on. "We're thinking of fixing this place up. It's already planned."

The girl looks doubtful, puts her own small smooth hand up to stroke a kitten which pushes under a torn piece of screen sagging limply from an open window.

"Paint and everything," Mrs. Domingo says.

"Then I can mention that in my report. That's good."

They walk over to the old adobe walls of the unfinished house. Mrs. Domingo never passes by without touching those walls, caressing their roughness, fingering the bits of straw still in the adobe.

"This is our real house, this one," Mrs. Domingo says. "But it never got itself finished."

They glance up, shading their eyes from the sun that shines down where the roof should be. "It would have been a good house. Three rooms," Mrs. Domingo says.

Sue Mills writes in her notebook. "Maybe I could call it a three-room house under construction."

Mrs. Domingo shrugs.

"When was this house started? I should mention that too."

"Twenty-three years ago."

"Well, perhaps I should just say *under construction.*"

It doesn't matter to Elma Domingo. To her it's simply The House. They walk back toward the two-room shack and stand facing it. It's so quiet here now without the children, Mrs. Domingo feels lonely. A social worker is not much for company, she thinks, still looking straight ahead.

"Now that's how many people in these two rooms, Mrs. Domingo?"

"Who says they're all in there at the same time?"

"Well, *if* they are, how many?"

"To tell the truth, I never counted them up. I never thought of it."

"Would you count them up now, Mrs. Domingo?"

"Anyway, some sleep down in the swimming pool. And now that it's so hot, of course some sleep outside by the mesquite tree. Should I go counting in all those places?"

Sue Mills nods. "If you would. And then let me know." She begins to write, chews her orange pen, writes again very very slowly. "Another thing, Mrs. Domingo. For that many children I'm sure we ought to be able to say you have two bedrooms at the very least."

"But this little house here — that's two rooms. You can sure count those rooms in if you want to. Two."

"But are they *bedrooms?* Don't you cook in there too?"

"Sure, we cook in there. But there are beds all around."

"See, Mrs. Domingo, there's not supposed to be cooking in a sleeping room."

"No?" Well, her ancestors out there in the desert didn't know that either. "I got to remember that," she says.

"It would be just wonderful if in your remodeling you could build another bedroom. Then you'd have one for the boys and one for the girls."

"That's better, huh?"

"Well . . . yes."

Mrs. Domingo shakes her head. There's so much to remember, so many rules. You don't know whether to act like they make sense or not. It's like talking to a crazy person . . . like talking to Lupe.

The girl is walking back and forth, squinting in the sun. "That pool, Mrs. Domingo . . . whatever is under all that? It really is a pool? An empty pool?"

"Sure." Mrs. Domingo isn't going to explain everything in the world to this girl. "A swimming pool."

"Could I possibly have a look down there? It might help if I could mention it in my report, but I don't know quite how to . . . ."

So they walk over to the door and Mrs. Domingo pulls it open. "You have to go down backwards." She waits for the girl to go in and disappear down the blue steps.

There is a thin mattress at the shallow end. "Careful," Mrs. Domingo calls down to her. "You can't stand up very well right there. It's a real good place for sleeping though."

In the deep end, Maria and Manny sit in the two straight chairs which have had the front legs shortened so they now rest fairly steadily against the slope of the pool. In the dim light it takes a minute or two before the girl can see. A chicken steps daintily over the two sleeping figures — Rose and Lopez, their heads slanting downward, arms wide apart for balance — and moves toward the social worker. Maria and Manny do not look up. They sit there formally, sit there looking into space, straight, silent, unmoving. Sue Mills turns quickly away, moves back toward the steps.

"Of course there's still a lot to be done," Mrs. Domingo says. "Someday we might get a real long electric cord so we could hang a light down from outside. Some people say we could even hook up a TV."

The girl is back up the blue steps even before Mrs. Domingo has started down.

"Well," Sue Mills says. "My . . . !"

Mrs. Domingo follows her slowly, slowly. Outside in the sunlight they look again at those papers, the white one and the yellow one. The girl is very quiet now, very thoughtful. Finally she says, "How about this? Two-room house with separate recreation room . . . ."

Now Mrs. Domingo is willing to smile at the girl a little. Not much, but a little — the way you'd smile at a foolish child who still has much to learn. Of course, that's the way it is with so many of these Anglos who tell people what the rules are; they may know the rules all right, but they don't know anything else. You almost feel sorry for them the way they make such a fuss over things that don't matter at all. "Recreation room . . . or maybe family room. And I'll be sure to mention that you're making some repairs."

"Many repairs," Mrs. Domingo says.

Sue Mills nods. "Extensive repairs. That's what I'm saying."

Mrs. Domingo stands in the shade and watches as the girl drives away. As soon as she is out of sight, the children begin peering around the greasewood bushes in the vacant lot. By the time she is a block away, they are all back asking, "Is it okay?"

Rose and Lopez come up from the swimming pool, still sleepy, blinking in the sun, worried. Maria and Manny stand beside them and Ignacio comes around the corner of the shack. Maria's two oldest girls, Anna and Amelia, run across the alley. They've been hiding behind the abandoned car, listening.

Everybody gathers now, slowly, casually, as though they just happened to be passing the palo verde tree, pausing for a moment in its thin shade.

"I'll tell you what," Mrs. Domingo says. "It would be a very good thing if we could find that boy that paints so pretty and he would come over here and put a lot of paint on this place." She lifts her hand toward the two-room shack. "A lot of paint to cover the boards and tin and everything."

"What color?" one of the children asks.

"Maybe blue. Maybe yellow. Pink would be okay. Green."

"I'll go get that boy then," Anna says. "I know where he is—hiding over at the Gomez place, but he can't come out until dark."

There are always boys in hiding, living at somebody else's house, avoiding probation officers, schools, police, foster homes . . . anything that traps you. Mrs. Domingo doesn't remember what this one, this Gabriel, is hiding from, but she wouldn't want him to take a chance on getting caught. "Tell him to come down the alley," she calls after Anna. "Tell him to be careful."

Then Mrs. Domingo turns to the rest of them. "We got to get a little money for some paint."

"I go to work for a lady tomorrow," Maria says. "I could give some."

But Manny and Lopez and Ignacio, the three men, shake their heads.

"Forget it," Manny says. "We'll go find paint. We'll get it today."

"You got money?"

"We'll find some that somebody isn't using. We'll look around."

Ignacio puts on his straw hat and goes in one direction, Lopez in another, but Mrs. Domingo signals Manny to wait. She wants to talk to him. First, however, she puts the children to work carrying rocks to make a border around the house, a little mound three or four inches high. Even stones lining the path to the outhouse, the path to the woodpile. Then she comes back to the shade and Manny and Maria follow her.

"I'll tell you this other rule they got. Maybe you can figure something out."

"He can," Maria says.

"This house is not supposed to be just any two rooms. It's supposed to be two *bedrooms.*" She says it slowly as though she herself isn't sure what the words mean.

Maria doesn't understand it either. "But people do sleep in both of those rooms."

"Sure, I told her that. But the rule says you got to sleep in rooms just made for sleeping. No stove or sink. No kitchen stuff. I guess that's it."

The children are listening too as they carry rocks. Amelia calls to them, "What if you said the stove wasn't really for cooking, just to keep warm with?"

Manny shakes his head. "No use. If they got that rule, you can't make them change it."

They walk over to the house; open the door, stare in at the old stove with the pot of beans on it, the table with the tin coffee cups and the plate of tortillas and the bowl of ground red chiles and the sugar. The boxes turned to sit on. The pots and pans hanging on the wall. The buckets for carrying water. The large round washtub for bathing. The shrine with its lighted candles, its paper flowers. The cigar box nailed to the wall for important papers. The three sagging beds, the mattresses on the dirt floor. The old refrigerator with the door propped open, a place for storing flour and beans and lard and coffee.

"Two bedrooms, eh?" Manny ponders it.

Mrs. Domingo repeats it. "Two. They aren't supposed to sleep in the same room . . . the girls and the boys." She shrugs.

"Even the babies?" Maria asks.

"Anybody," Mrs. Domingo says. "Any age."

They smile.

"Listen," Manny says. "You just got to think of that rule. No matter how crazy. Just think of that rule and we'll find some way to beat it."

They walk slowly around the house, back out the front door, over to the mesquite tree.

"Sure," Manny says. "You just take the stove and the icebox outside."

"Then we got no kitchen."

"No, but there's no rule says you got to have a kitchen. Then at least you got you a two-bedroom house."

So it is settled. "I never minded cooking outside anyway," Mrs. Domingo says.

Manny and Rose and Maria begin pulling the stove across the dirt floor and out the door, getting the stovepipe down, dragging out the boxes of pots and pans, the refrigerator. All this goes under the ramada now, under the trees. Anywhere.

"What about the table? Can you have a table in a bedroom?"

"No, I don't think so," Manny decides. "Just beds. Nothing but where they're going to sleep. Boys and girls . . . ."

"And the saints," Mrs. Domingo says. "I know it's okay to have saints in there."

The artist, Gabriel, arrives while they are still bringing out boxes of dishes. He doesn't want to wait until night after all. Somebody drives him over in a red Ford and they wheel around the corner in a haze of exhaust smoke and the rumbling noise of a dragging muffler. The car roars through the alley, stops by the woodpile. When the dust settles, two boys crawl under the car to tie the muffler up again with a piece of wire from the neighbor's fence while another raises the hood and unscrews the radiator cap. Gabriel gets out and the children all put down their rocks and come to stand beside him.

He looks at the tin and plywood and cardboard of that shack and shakes his head and laughs. "They're going to say you're crazy to try to paint up that pile of junk. Man, you need a lot more than paint."

Mrs. Domingo gives him a straight old-lady stare, acts as though she had not heard him. She wants more respect from the young ones, doesn't like to see Papago boys acting like Anglos — not speaking properly to their elders. She makes him wait for awhile before she speaks to him.

"You an artist?"

"I can paint any picture," Gabriel says. "Give me anything to copy, a postcard or a holy picture or a girl or mountains and cactus."

"Which ones do you do best?"

"Holy pictures, I guess." He spits in the dust. "That or girls."

Mrs. Domingo points with her mesquite stick to a large piece of tin wired to the wall near the door — a faint white and red reminder that it was once part of an advertisement for chewing tobacco.

"That would be a good place for a picture," Mrs. Domingo tells him. She backs off and squints. "Most of the boards will just be painted, maybe blue ... whatever colors they find around today. But it would be a very pretty thing to have some real pictures too."

Gabriel stands back considering the project, hands deep in the pockets of his skintight levis. He slowly ties his unbuttoned flowered shirt at the waist, lights a cigarette and nods. "I did the Garden of Gethsemane for my mother for Christmas and once I did St. Teresa for my probation officer."

One of the boys gets up from under the car and comes over and kicks at the cardboard walls of the house. "He does horses good too," he tells them. "Maybe he could put some way back behind the Jesus or something."

Mrs. Domingo goes inside, comes out again with a 1958 calendar of religious pictures. "I wonder what they'd like."

Everybody looks at the pictures. Mrs. Domingo keeps coming back to St. Martin cutting his cloak in two with a sword, wrapping half of the red scrap around the shoulders of a beggar—almost naked, poor man.

"That's dumb," the children keep saying. "Now he's ruined his coat and the naked guy is still cold with just that rag around him."

Even so, there is a fine prancing white horse which St. Martin is riding and this is a good saint for the poor. Everybody knows that.

St. Martin then.

Gabriel sharpens his pencil with a green switchblade knife, props the calendar up against the wall, and begins to draw on the tin.

"I still don't think it's going to do any good," he says.

"You do it anyway," Mrs. Domingo says quietly. "We got to try."

"Okay."

"And remember, you've always got this for a place to come to any time you got to hide from somebody."

"Thank you very much." He is polite now, treating her as an old woman should be treated.

"How about house numbers?" she asks him. "Can you paint them very pretty over the door?"

"Sure I can. But it's not going to do any good."

Now Mrs. Domingo walks away from all of them, walks down the street to her old friend, Jude. Saint of the impossible. Staring straight ahead, as always. A little dusty, a little faded.

The thing is, she tells him, we don't know yet just exactly what those rules are. We don't know what we have to do to keep Lupe's kids. But maybe the little paths will help, and of course we'll rake the dirt nice and smooth. And then the paint. White people always like a painted house.

What's your suggestion, Jude?

She walks home across the vacant lots, down the dusty alleys. Her old feet prefer the feeling of earth under them, not sidewalks. Not cement.

CHAPTER 9

GABRIEL SOTO

He's a young deer hiding in any rocky canyon, raising his head to listen, the skin along his backbone twitching. He sniffs the wind, the still air, sniffs danger. Yes, but he's in town and what he runs from is cops and schools and foster homes.

Even in his tight levis and flowered shirt and shiny shoes he feels naked. Feels himself a weed, a stone, a deer, a handful of earth. Feels himself Indian. That's it more than anything else . . . *Indian*. Wild beautiful Indian. Fierce young mountain Indian. Gabriel Soto forgets he even speaks English.

He's wearing a beaded headband with a feather, just a turkey feather, stuck in it. Every day when he comes to paint the tin wall of Mrs. Domingo's shack he sees her looking at that headband.

Today, finally, she stands holding her cup of coffee and peers down at him.

"That thing around your head. What's that supposed to be?"

"That's my headband. What you *think* it is?"

"Is it supposed to be an Indian thing?"

"Sure it's an Indian thing."

She turns her head sideways, studying the design of yellow and purple flowers, all beads. "What kind of Indian? Apache?"

"Just Indian."

She shakes her head, doesn't say anything. He finally has to ask her, "What about it?"

Mrs. Domingo takes a breath. "Your grandfather, he was a very good farmer way out around Baboquivari Mountain. His father, he lived over by Crowhang. He was a singer for his village. Now those were Papago men."

"Well, I know that." He puts his paintbrush down and studies her face to find out what she is telling him. "I'm as Papago as them."

"Well, they didn't wear things tied around their heads. They didn't wear beads either."

The children look at Gabriel, waiting for him to answer. He only shrugs and grins. "So?"

But after awhile when Mrs. Domingo has gone back to her cooking under the ramada, he calls to her, "Okay, what did they wear then?"

"Not much. In the old days, maybe sandals made out of hide. A little something wrapped around the waist. No movie Indian stuff."

"I bet they wore feathers," Gabriel says.

"Sure," Maria's boy, Errol Flynn, agrees.

"You town boys! Listen, they had eagle feathers for prayers and visions. The medicine man had feathers . . . feathers on shields. But not just feathers to stick in anybody's hair."

"Well, it's a later time," Gabriel says. "Things have changed. And anyway I'm as Indian as you old guys are."

"You are. In your blood you are."

Gabriel himself has never lived on the reservation. He's only been there five or ten times in his life and then for no more than a few days. A visitor, an outsider. All he remembers are the ocotillo fences around the mud houses, the quiet, quiet hills. He remembers an old man showing him mounds of heavy grey boulders on a mountainside and telling him that his ancestors lay under those rocks. Something about leaving a plate of beans and a tin spoon and a candle there on the rocks, presents for the dead. A prayer feather tied to a little stick. He remembers the taste of cholla buds too.

But he doesn't know the language. Just a few phrases, forty or fifty words that the town Indians mix with English and Spanish.

Even so, he *knows* himself Indian. Sees himself a tall plains Indian on a fast pony. Not walking the rocky Papago desert. Sees himself a Navajo with turquoise around his neck and dangling from his ears and heavy on his fingers. Not Papago poor without a thing to shine against his skin. Of course when he was little, the Mexican kids and the white kids and the black kids all teased the Indians. In those days he always hoped people would think he was Mexican. But now . . . now he sees himself dancing a war dance at dawn (god*damn* he wishes he knew that language), chanting songs for power and strength and visions. Not standing around some broken-down car listening to cowboy songs.

"You ever heard of Red Power?" he asks Mrs. Domingo.

"No." The old woman shakes her head. "Not that. Or if I did I forgot what it means."

He snaps his fingers to the electric guitar music of his transistor radio. "You better remember what it means. Everybody knows about that."

"I know," says Errol Flynn Vasquez.

"Me too," says Anna. "It's written on the wall over by the secondhand store."

"There's going to be a meeting about Red Power. And man, I'm going to that meeting."

"Red Power," the youngest ones repeat. They like whatever Gabriel likes.

Gabriel has been painting the St. Martin picture for two days now. He's copied the one from the religious calendar, has added high pink desert mountains to the background. And he has made St. Martin's fat white horse a pinto. He likes to paint bucking horses, wants to make old St. Martin hang on like a rodeo rider, but after all, Martin has enough to do trying to slice a cloak in half with his sword. At least he makes the horse rear up a little on his hind legs.

He's just stopped to roll a cigarette when the new young social worker walks up to the gate — Sue Mills, the one who told Mrs. Domingo she'd have to fix up her house, the one who smiles so much. She waves to Mrs. Domingo as she comes near, bounces, almost runs, a little-girl motion no Papago woman uses.

She starts to speak to Mrs. Domingo, notices the painting. "Oh, look," she cries out. "Just look."

The children stand beside Gabriel proudly. He barely glances up.

"You like it okay?" Mrs. Domingo asks.

"I love it," Sue Mills says. "I just hope the health department will too. Who is it?"

"St. Martin," Mrs. Domingo says and points to the calendar. "See, he's cutting his coat in two so the beggar can have half." She sounds uncertain.

Sue Mills seems puzzled too. She kneels down in the sand beside Gabriel and peers at the scene. "I don't know too much about which saint does what."

"It sure will make the house look better," Mrs. Domingo says.

But Sue Mills is watching Gabriel's face. "You're a good artist. Really good. Have you had lessons somewhere?"

"Not me."

"You should go to art school." She runs her fingers through her long blonde hair, moves back into the shade of the house.

When Gabriel doesn't answer, she says, "Really, you should." And she looks at Mrs. Domingo for agreement. "Shouldn't he?"

Mrs. Domingo raises her hands. "If he's good already why does he need to go to school?"

White people are always thinking of some kind of school. Lessons for everything. It's a wonder they don't have lessons for learning to breathe.

The girl turns back to Gabriel. "Of course, *honestly*, you should be painting out of your Indian heritage . . . pictures that would be a part of your own culture." She lifts one leg at a time, wiggles her bare pink toes to shake the sand out of her sandals. They all watch her; it's like a dance.

There is sudden tenderness and emotion in her voice. "I feel very strongly about it," she says, moving closer to Gabriel again. "I wish the young Indian people like you would just follow their own tribal beliefs. You know, keep the old ways and . . . be true to themselves." She's breathless.

Mrs. Domingo raises her head in surprise but Gabriel only nods.

"I do that," he says. "Almost everything I draw is Indian stuff."

The children come closer, want to touch anything pretty . . . the long pale hair, the blue dress, the turquoise rings.

Anna says, "He paints cowboy horses good too. And girls."

"Girls." The children have seen his girls. They cover their faces with their hands and giggle.

But Gabriel says, "Almost everything I draw is Indian."

Sue Mills nods. "I know how you must feel," she says. She speaks very tenderly to Gabriel, whispering almost. The children come still closer to listen, to watch.

"Oh, what's your name? Nobody told me."

"Flaming Arrow," he says.

She sucks in her breath . . . a sound of delight. "Flaming Arrow *what?*"

"Flaming Arrow Gonzales," he says. He does not even have to pause to think of that name. And it's a fine one. He's pleased with it.

The children like the name too. You can tell by their faces. After all, they know that it is often necessary to make up the names you give to Anglos, and they are silent, serious, watching to see if the pretty white girl is going to believe Gabriel.

"I'm so glad you use your real Indian name," she says. "That's what I'd do if I were Indian."

"Yeah."

Gabriel goes back to painting, doesn't even glance up at this girl. Doesn't want to talk to her any more. He has too many secrets and any social worker is as dangerous as a cop. Never mind if she does have yellow hair and three Indian rings on her fingers. Never mind if her tiny nipples show through her blue dress.

She stays there watching him paint, leaning sideways into the thin line of shade that reaches out from the house. Mrs. Domingo comes and goes but Sue Mills hardly notices her.

"Honestly, Flaming Arrow, I think there are people in this town who ought to know there's a talented Papago artist down here. Somebody important ought to know. Then maybe you could go to art school. Anything . . . ."

"That's okay. Forget it."

"Think of the inspiration you'd be to other Indians."

He shrugs, spits in the dust.

"In a way you owe it to your people. Honestly."

Gabriel won't look at her. Acts as though he hasn't heard anything she's saying. He paints very slowly, bending toward his work, all his attention on the flaring nostrils of St. Martin's pinto horse. The horse seems to be turning his head to glare fiercely at the beggar, that poor surprised man.

Sue Mills keeps talking to Gabriel, murmuring excitedly even though he does not look at her.

"You're just awfully modest, Flaming Arrow. That's your trouble. And I know that's how Indians are, but I want everybody to hear about you."

111

"Not me," he says. "Not a chance."

He's ready to run. Ready to beat it for another town. Maybe out to one of his uncles on the reservation. Jesus, he's as good as back in juvenile detention if she keeps this up. Can't you just see her hauling people down here to see him? Probation officers, judges, cops. The whole works.

"Maybe a newspaper story with pictures of your paintings."

Mrs. Domingo tries to come to his rescue. "This is a very shy boy here. He don't want people coming to see him. This boy, he never even talks to strangers."

"We'll see," the social worker says, smiling. Her hands move toward Gabriel as though she wants to touch him but she grasps her papers instead.

At least he can outrun her, he thinks.

Gabriel knows the back alleys. He knows the hiding places. He knows whose door will open to him when he stands there shivering in the middle of the night. God knows, he's had practice at running, at hiding like a desert animal. Why should man be different from his rabbit brothers, his coyote brothers, his pack rat brothers, his prairie dog brothers, just because he's moved to town?

Oh yes, he runs, but still it's with a certain amount of joy. Even when he's running away, he runs free, he goes easy as a tumbleweed. You wouldn't know he's ever in a hurry.

He's seventeen now and nothing surprises him much. Good luck or bad, he figures he's had each one in almost equal amounts. Maybe even more good than bad. That's better than many a coyote has, many a man too.

The good luck. That's the check he gets every month from welfare.

All the Indians in South Tucson know about that check and nobody begrudges Gabriel his good luck. Hasn't he had a party every month on the day that money comes? Bought frijoles for many a family, put up bail for somebody, helped out when a car was being repossessed, bought candies for a funeral? Hasn't he bought wine and marijuana and beer? Not only that, he gives his grandmother $9.50 a month so she can have a telephone. A quarter to the church every month too. He doesn't stay for mass, just strolls in and tosses his quarter clinking into the poor box.

That check! The town Indians smile and shake their heads whenever it is mentioned. Old people chuckle when they see Gabriel go by. It's everybody's only joke on welfare. A good joke too. And part of the joke is that Gabriel enjoys himself. That's something *welfare* doesn't like — somebody having a good time.

Of course that check is a mistake. Think of those important white people sitting there at their desks with all their papers and rule books and typewriters and pens making a mistake and sending some wild Indian kid a check. But it's been coming for almost two years now. It arrives even when he's locked up for joy riding or drinking or ditching school or running away from one of those foster homes. It comes even when he's over around Yuma picking oranges. Every month, $37.50 lying there in the mailbox at his grandmother's place. Who knows why? But people say, "Well welfare does crazier things than that." The difference is that most of the other things are unpleasant. For once, something nice, something to enjoy.

Gabriel himself simply accepts the check as good luck just the way he accepts being locked up once in a while as bad luck.

Bad luck. Well, he was born in one of those rotting southside trailer courts where the trailers will never move again, they've sunk so far down into the earth. There his skinny dark mother drank and wept and whored and coughed up blood. She was thirty-two when she died and by that time Gabriel was already on his own. He hadn't seen her for months.

He doesn't think of that as bad luck. No, the bad luck was school. Getting thrown out for ditching. That brought the authorities around looking for him, got his name on their papers. That was the bad luck . . . letting them get his name.

White people say you have to let them shut you up in their schools *every* day, *every* day, *every* day. But if you can't stand it and you miss a few days, how do they punish you? By saying you can't go back to school. Stay away from here, you bad kid. Now that seems like a crazy punishment if what they wanted so bad in the first place was for you to stay in school. There's no use trying to figure it out. An Indian can't understand that kind of thinking.

When they started checking up on him, going from door to door to find him, that was bad luck. When they discovered his mother was dead and there wasn't any father around and he was living here and there . . . that was bad luck. It's true he was with his own grandmother part of the time or with other Indians who had known his mother. But white people make such a fuss over where a person is supposed to sleep. They have so many rules about it. This particular house. This room. This time of night.

When those people start after you, there's nothing to do but run. Only a fool would stand still and wait for them. But then when they find you, they bring you to Court and call you a runaway. That's another crime against you.

So Gabriel knows foster homes with white people who write the rules of the house on a piece of paper and put it up in the kitchen and he knows the jail they call juvenile detention . . . and they are bad luck too.

Right now there's a little thing about joy riding in a stolen car, a new yellow Mustang. Such a pretty thing, how could you resist getting behind the wheel? That yellow car full of Papago kids whizzing through the alleys for an hour, everybody singing, waving, drinking. Even picking up the winos and the children, giving them a ride. Radio blasting.

Well, now they're looking for Gabriel again, so he has to be careful. Thinks he might go harvesting cantaloupes over in California for awhile. Maybe over to the lettuce fields. But he can hide right here at home if he wants to. In this part of town any Indian can hide from any white man who comes from the other side of town. The Anglos stand out here and people notice them even if nobody looks up or glances their way. And of course nobody will tell those people anything.

Even his grandmother only shakes her head, squints up at them as though Gabriel Soto is a name she may have heard once but she can't quite remember where. "Him? He could be on the reservation. That could be it. Or if not there . . . ."

"Would you know where he gets his mail?"

"But who would write to him?"

She shakes her head. Shrugs.

Gabriel doesn't think even his last probation officer would recognize him now anyway. He's taller and his hair has grown almost to his shoulders, and he thinks *Indian* whenever he sees himself in a mirror. *Indian.* That word has begun to move through him, stirring, alive. He believes it's given him a different look.

And when Sue Mills looks at him now, Gabriel can tell she's thinking it too. *Indian.*

"Listen, Flaming Arrow, it's been just wonderful watching you paint. But how can I get in touch with you?"

Suddenly he's a deer again hiding at the mouth of that rocky canyon. Looking over his shoulder.

"I have to be out of town for a while," he says. "Somebody's real sick."

"But I want to see your other artwork."

"Somebody stole it."

She looks distressed.

"Then let me bring you art materials," she says. "Whatever you need. I'll buy you paints."

Gabriel is uneasy. "I'm joining the army pretty soon anyway. I guess I won't have time to paint."

She shakes her head. Again her hands move toward him.

"I'm already signed up," he says. "It could be tomorrow. Any day."

The children look from one to another, their round faces closed.

"At least let's talk before you go," she says. "Your art career is so important I want to do something. I want . . . ." Her words hang there in the afternoon.

Gabriel stands up, stretches, doesn't say anything. He's jumpy. Wants to get away. Now. Now.

Mrs. Domingo comes back, hangs her bird cage in the chinaberry tree, draws Sue Mills away from Gabriel by saying, "These birds came from Mexico. From Guaymas." So the girl walks over to the tree but she keeps looking around until she can see Gabriel again.

She writes a number on a piece of paper, goes back and hands it to Gabriel. "You can phone me at the office in the morning."

"Yeah." He sticks the paper in his pocket without looking at it. Leans against the house. Waits.

As soon as she is gone he says, "Shit."

"You're an Indian artist," the children say. "You are."

He grins again.

"Well, what about it?" Mrs. Domingo asks him. "You going to finish painting this place or you going to hide out?"

He thinks it over, doesn't answer yet. Just climbs up on a box and over the front door of the shack he paints in large flowing letters: *RED POWER*.

The children who can read, Anna and Errol Flynn and Jane and Rose's oldest girl, Flora, all call out the words. But Lupe's two get it wrong and yell out, "Red flower!"

Gabriel tells Mrs. Domingo, "Don't worry. I'll finish up St. Martin tomorrow and I'll do another picture – an Indian one – on that piece of tin on the other side. That way if anybody drives up they won't see me. But I'd better not be hanging around too long."

Mrs. Domingo nods. She hands him tortillas wrapped in brown paper to take with him, pats his arm.

"The white lady loves him," the children say giggling. "You can tell she does."

Already eating one of the tortillas, Gabriel peers out into the street, doesn't see any strange car, goes off down the alley whistling.

The place he goes now is his grandmother's house. The old lady with the telephone. It's a princess phone, pink as a cactus flower. Beautiful.

That telephone sits on a crocheted doily in the center of the table and the three chairs are drawn up around it so that whoever comes into the house sits facing the telephone. It's like a living thing, a person who waits silent and brooding through long silences and then comes to life.

Everyone knows that Gabriel gives Mrs. Belen money from his welfare check for that telephone. What a fine grandson! No matter what else he does, he's a good boy. And Gabriel himself feels proud whenever he goes into the house.

The house is one room, a shed built onto the back of the Chinese grocery store. The only furniture besides the table and the three chairs is an iron bed and a wood-burning cook stove.

The chairs are old and unsteady. The table is rough and the bed sags under its grey quilt. Linoleum from the city dump has been laid across the dirt floor, three or four pieces of it, no patterns left, only the imprint of years of footsteps. You can't tell what color it used to be.

Only the telephone is a color. Only the telephone is bright and new and clean and beautiful.

Barefooted, old Mrs. Belen sits looking at it, smiles, gets up and hobbles over to the beans. She moves the coffee pot back a little, returns to the chair by the telephone.

Gabriel doesn't have to knock here, just comes in. The old woman doesn't ask if he wants food. She just puts a plate of beans before him on the table.

"You want to phone somebody," she asks. "Go ahead. You got the number?"

"No. I'm just passing by."

"Nobody after you, huh?"

"Not right now."

"Then use the phone."

"Later," he says. "Listen, I may go over to Yuma for awhile. Or maybe join the army." He bends over his plate of beans, glances up to see how the old woman takes the news.

She sits watching him eat, doesn't speak again until he has finished. She herself has a cup of coffee.

"Maybe the army," he says.

"Why?"

"I just thought of it today."

She shakes her head. "You shouldn't be trying to go and get killed. Not before you get some babies for me to take care of."

"Who says I want to get killed? Papagos were wild fighters. They were the great warriors."

His grandmother looks surprised. *Papagos?*

"Sure."

"But they didn't want to fight. Not them." She chuckles. "Sometimes the Apaches made them fight. Apaches. They were the fighters. It's the Apaches ought to go to the army."

"Well, the Papagos won, didn't they?"

"Sometimes they did. But our people always had to use a lot of magic to help them. I guess they used to sing those special songs all night before a battle. And they had to fast, too."

"Man!"

"And when a Papago killed one of the enemy then he was out of it. He had to leave the battle."

"How come?"

"He had to make himself pure again. He had to be alone for sixteen days and all that time he had to fast and do certain magic things before he could come back."

"You mean he had to clear out while the fight was still going on?"

"Sure."

"Some way to fight," Gabriel says.

Mrs. Belen smiles. "You town kids don't know a thing about the old ways."

"I'm still Indian," Gabriel says. "Listen, I'm as Indian as you are."

She puts more frijoles on his plate. "You want to sleep here tonight?"

"No, but if anybody comes around looking for me, remember, you don't know." He sprinkles dried red chiles over the beans as he talks. "Even if it's a girl, a white girl . . . you don't know."

She nods.

When he's leaning against the door, peering out to see who is in the alley, his grandmother says, "If you go to the army then how about when your check comes to the mailbox? You wouldn't be able to get it. How could I cash that paper to pay money for the telephone?"

"Yeah. . . ."

"I sure like my pink phone."

Gabriel knows that. Before the telephone this old woman spent most of her time alone. Sometimes another old woman hobbled down the dusty alley or somebody's daughter brought tamales. But not often. Not often.

Now there are people at the door all day. All they have to say is, "Hi, Miz Belen." And they come in and stand there a minute, maybe even sit down at the table within an inch of the phone, and then as though the thought just came to them, they say, "How about if I use your phone, okay?"

It's the teenage kids who come to use the phone more than the older people. The numbers they call are written in pencil there on the wall. City jail. County jail. Movies. Bars. Mrs. Belen herself does not get calls. Who would she know with a telephone? Only the priest, but you don't call the priest to pass the time of day.

She enjoys the telephone just the same. When it rings she shouts into it, "Bueno? . . . Allo?" And she takes messages to be repeated later. Who had better keep out of sight, who is sick or dying, who is in jail.

"I sure like my phone all right."

"Okay," Gabriel says. "I guess I better not go to the army so you can keep it."

On his way out he asks her, "You know what Red Power means?"

She shakes her head.

"Well, the young ones do." He touches his headband. The turkey feather has fallen out.

He goes out into the evening heat, walks whistling toward the part of town where they'll be music and dancing and beer and where his friends will be waiting for him. Doesn't know yet where he'll sleep tonight. Wishes he could be like a deer, curling his body into a clump of weeds, maybe under a manzanita bush in the hills, maybe in some sandy wash. He'd like that. But the only weeds around here are in some vacant lot and you'd be lying on broken glass from a thousand wine bottles and the cops would nab you. They'd find the law that says you can't sleep on broken glass and weeds in a vacant lot. There's bound to be one. Man, there's a law against everything.

CHAPTER 10

MARIA VASQUEZ

White people give such importance to houses. They honor their houses more than they honor their ancestors. They make such a fuss over everything about a house . . . water and toilet and electric lights and screens. They ask so many questions about a house. Who comes under its roof? Who sleeps there besides you? Whose children nestle together on the blankets on the floor?

Maria remembers enough of her childhood on the reservation to know that there a house was a thing of no importance at all. There were so many things that mattered more: the sahuaro fruit harvest, songs and ceremonies and dances, corn and squash ripening, mesquite beans being dried for winter, old men singing their own planting songs, telling the same Papago stories year after year in the darkness of winter nights so that every child would know how Earthmaker took a little dirt from his skin and rolled it in his hand and made a ball of it and let a greasewood bush grow out of that ball of earth to make a world. All these things make you feel safe. Not your house. People would have thought you a fool to care so much about a house.

Now *land.* That is something to care about. There's a good Papago word for that — *Tohono,* desert land. You think of rocks and weeds and dry grasses and hills and arroyos. The great mountain, Baboquivari, rising up for Papagos to turn their faces to.

The land is important. Your well-being, your strength, is in land. Not in houses. Never houses. Like any desert creature's burrow, a house could be changed any time, one for another. One for dry times of the year when it was cold and there was not as much food and families might go to the hills to hunt. Another for the rainy time when the cactus was in fruit on the south side of the hills where they say Coyote scattered the seeds for his people, the Papagos. Any house would do, any shade, any shelter from the sun and rain. And wouldn't people have laughed if a man had built himself a bigger house than he needed!

On the reservation you grew up seeing the little rock shelters high in the ledges of the mountains where your ancestors chased out foxes and coyotes and mountain lions to make their own hard sleeping places. You saw where the smoke from their fires had blackened the rocks overhead. You found the ashes of those fires still in the sand and the tiny bones of their rabbit stews still whitening in the sun.

Out there walking the same rocky land, you live so close to your ancestors that their lives never seem far away from you. Even their ways of living in caves and cliffs seems natural enough. You couldn't mind so much living like that. As good as an alley in town anyway.

But of course here in town with the Anglos you have to think in a different way. In their way.

Maria is trying to do that now . . . to think in *their* way. "But I still got me an Indian mind," she says. "It won't think White. It thinks Indian."

"Mine too," Rose says. "That's our trouble."

They are sitting under the chinaberry tree where Mrs. Domingo has hung her cage of finches. Every ten or fifteen minutes they walk around the other side of the shack where Gabriel is painting an Indian war scene on the tin wall. Papagos against Apaches, he says.

The day is fiercely hot, heat that moves against you, sinks into you, pushes against your eyes, creeps into your body when you take a breath. It's the heat that comes just before rain and the heaviness of the approaching storm passes slowly across the desert, up and down the streets. This time it won't be just a few drops, just the promise of rain. This is a storm. Even their bodies are expecting it, sense its nearness.

Maria knows she's going to have to go back across the alley to the yard of the condemned house and drag her mattresses away before the storm comes. But there is still an hour. You learn to know these rains as well as you know your lover.

The people who have gathered to watch Gabriel paint watch the sky too. Everyone who passes comes over to see the new picture. All the children are there beside him, Maria's and Rose's and Lupe's and five or six others too. They not only admire the painting, they admire Gabriel, beautiful in his tight pants and flowered shirt open to the waist, his beaded headband.

Only Rose and Maria are sitting away from the others. They've sat so often together like this, not speaking for five or ten minutes at a time yet knowing that their thoughts are following the same long path.

"Maybe it's going to be all right," Rose says.

"Maybe." Maria knows it is not good to hope for too much. That's tempting bad luck. Even so, she feels bolder these days when Manny is around. She does feel that maybe . . . *maybe* . . . things will be better.

Manny has gone to chop cotton today to try to get four or five dollars to make a payment on his mail-order detective course.

But Maria reminds herself that even Manny, smart as he is, doesn't know Anglo rules until he hears one. They always come as a surprise even to him. Nothing you can prepare for beforehand.

"One thing," Maria says. "My social worker is supposed to think my kids live here. And that other social worker is supposed to think Lupe's kids live here. And yours is supposed to think you live here. But what if they all come at the same time?"

Rose shrugs. "Maybe they never will come here the same day."

They sit in silence for a long time.

"It would sure be dumb for just Ignacio and those little kids to have two rooms. Such little kids. You could fit them in anywhere. They don't take up enough space for two rooms."

Maria doesn't want to think about it now. Later when Manny is back it will be all right because he takes pleasure in trying to unravel these puzzles. He lets them roll around in his mind until they begin to make sense, however long that takes. Sometimes at night lying beside him on the mattress in the yard she knows he is still searching for some answer and she is content to wait until he finds it. Just let her touch him. Just let her hands rest on his great brown hill of a belly.

Now that is a better thought . . . Manny's belly. Maria lets herself enjoy it now, half closes her eyes. You can't really think of a man's belly with your eyes open. You have to go soft. Then you can almost remember the breathing, the motion as even as waves. She's never seen a wave, but she's felt the ocean in a man's breathing . . . .

"Hey!" It's Rose. "Who's that white woman?"

A car has stopped at the curb. Maria gasps as she watches Mrs. Waterman pulling herself wearily out. The woman leans against the car door. You can see she's hot, tired.

Dear God, so that's my punishment for sitting here taking too much pleasure in my thoughts. That's my notice to say a rosary once in a while instead of thinking of a naked man.

Maria still doesn't move. "She's come to see the address," she whispers to Rose. "That's the one, the social worker." Her throat is dry.

Mrs. Domingo comes around the side of the house, sees Maria's face, knows who it is getting out of that white car.

"You got to act natural," Rose whispers.

Maria gets up slowly almost as though she hadn't noticed the white car at all. Without looking up she walks toward the fence and pulls open the sagging gate.

Somehow it is a surprise to see Mrs. Waterman standing up, away from her desk and out in the heat of the afternoon, away from her papers. No, she has brought some papers with her. For company, Maria thinks. That woman wouldn't go anywhere without her book of rules and three copies of everything.

The neighbors leave. The children move back. And on the other side of the shack Gabriel stops painting and leans forward, unseen, to listen.

"Well, Mrs. Vasquez . . . ." Her face is shiny with perspiration. She stops to look at the St. Martin painting but she sighs, does not show the same pleasure everyone else has felt over it.

"Is this . . . the house you've rented, Mrs. Vasquez?"

Maria nods. "It's 107 W. Santa Rufina. That's the address, just like I told you on the phone. 107."

It is certainly true that white people like numbers, addresses. An Indian seldom uses them. He'll say turn left by the ocotillo fence, go back behind the mountain and then follow the wash, stop at the house with the goat tied to the post. Even in town you'll go back and forth to a house for years without thinking to look at the number someone has put on it.

But Maria notices that Mrs. Waterman looks up immediately to find the number.

"It isn't written there," Maria says. "But it's on the mailbox in front. And we're going to paint it here on the house too. The number, it's going to be up over the door."

Now Mrs. Waterman peers sideways at the painting as though she can't quite bear to turn her full gaze that way. She sighs again.

"And nobody lives here except yourself and your four children. Is that correct?"

Maria nods.

Of course everybody knows that Maria has five children, not four, but welfare isn't supposed to know about the baby, Carmen. It was this very woman, this Mrs. Waterman, who had so definitely told Maria not to have another child.

Carmen is right there, sitting on the ground sucking on a tortilla. She's sleepy and dirty, almost ready to lie down somewhere. Mrs. Domingo has strolled over to the tree to dip some water out of the olla and she stands there by Rose. "You're having your house . . . painted?" Mrs. Waterman asks.

"Yes, that's it."

This time Mrs. Waterman looks straight toward St. Martin but she still shows no pleasure at all in the painting. None. "Of course painting pictures on the outside is not as important as keeping the inside clean, is it, Mrs. Vasquez."

"No, I guess not."

Mrs. Waterman goes to the door but she does not step into the darkness of the rooms.

"There seem to be a great many people around here," she says. The way she says it, it is a question.

Maria isn't sure she's going to be able to bring her voice up out of her throat at all, but it comes at last, very small and weak. "It sure is a crowded part of town."

Mrs. Waterman hesitates. You can tell she's tired standing in the heat. The thunder has begun to rumble far away, north of the mountains, and she keeps glancing toward the sky.

Very casually, Rose gets up and moves slowly across the yard and speaks to the children — her own and Lupe's — and they trail along behind her. Rose leads them past Maria and Mrs. Waterman on her way out the gate.

"I got to be going," Rose says to Maria. "It was nice to see you."

The children look solemnly toward Maria and Mrs. Waterman as they file through the gate.

"Come back again sometime," Maria tries to say. She isn't sure she can be heard. Then she says to Mrs. Waterman, "My friend came to pass the afternoon."

Mrs. Waterman takes off her glasses, wipes them on a handkerchief, puts them on again quickly as Rose turns around and comes back inside the yard and picks up Carmen and walks out the gate with Carmen sagging sleepily against her shoulder. This time Rose and Maria do not even glance toward each other.

Mrs. Waterman watches them go. "Almost forgot one of them," she says. Maria shrugs.

Mrs. Domingo, sitting under the ramada now, weaving a basket, never glances up. And Maria is looking down at the ground most of the time even as she stands there with Mrs. Waterman.

Maria can smell the rain coming closer, thinks of her mattresses lying there in the open. Surely Mrs. Waterman will leave in time for her to get them under cover. If they are ruined, those mattresses, there will be no hope of getting others. She knows that. St. Jude, good friend, can't you take this lady away? Or if not that, at least hold off the storm awhile. Either one.

"You'll receive a check then but that means . . . ," and Mrs. Waterman says it very clearly, "that means you must be providing a satisfactory home for your children and that you come down to sign nonsupport charges against your husband."

Maria feels her face reddening with shame. She hates for Mrs. Domingo and Gabriel and her own children to hear her pretend that she will sign those papers, the papers that would send poor Joe Vasquez to another jail.

"And again, Mrs. Vasquez, I must warn you that no man is to be living here with you."

"I know that," Maria whispers.

Mrs. Waterman puts her pen back in her purse, wipes her face again. "And I just hope you're making some plans, Mrs. Vasquez. I always try to emphasize that. You won't succeed unless you look ahead and decide what to aim for."

"Yes," Maria says.

As Mrs. Waterman walks slowly toward her car Gabriel peers around the house to have a look at her. He lifts his head and spits in her direction.

Maria begins to breathe again.

"I wouldn't even glance up at her," Gabriel says. "Shit." He goes back to his battle picture.

"Well, I got to glance at her. Either that or I'm going to have no place for my kids to sleep."

"You got no place now. Just sleeping in an empty yard. What's so fancy about that!"

"Yeah, but if they send a check maybe we'll have a place by the time the rains are really bad. Maybe."

Mrs. Domingo leaves her basket and walks past them into the shack to light a candle before the shrine which has been set up on top of a broken television.

And Maria goes across the alley. She walks slowly, unhurried, though the air has changed and the smell of the storm is like a wild bird in the air. Let the other things get wet. They've been wet before, but the mattresses are Maria's most expensive possessions. Six dollars each at the Salvation Army store.

But one of the mattresses is gone. The double one that she and Manny sleep on. Gone.

Maria doesn't move. She doesn't make a sound. She stands very still, hands on her hips. At first she just stares at the bare dusty place where the mattress was, doesn't want to know yet what else is gone, doesn't let her eyes move to the stove.

But the wind becomes stronger, slapping at her cotton dress. Dust in her eyes, stinging her face. Finally she lifts her head and looks over by the tree where the stove is. It's her tortilla pan she's worried about. Yes, it's gone. Her good heavy iron tortilla pan.

There's nothing to do but drag the other two mattresses one by one into Mrs. Domingo's yard.

"In here," Mrs. Domingo shouts.

The mattresses are so thin they fold and bend easily. It's no trouble getting both of them into the house.

"Just two?" Mrs. Domingo asks her.

Maria shakes her head. "One's gone. My tortilla pan too."

For a moment they let the mattresses sag there on the dirt floor. The two women stand looking at one another. But there are things to be done now. Other things to protect. The stove and the pots and pans and dishes that they had moved to the ramada last week have to be covered with something. Pieces of cardboard or tin will do. You expect things to get a little wet.

Rose and the children come back now. The children run but Rose walks the same way Maria walks, slowly, heavily. "I come back to visit a little more," Rose says. "Me and my kids." They all smile, the children too.

Gabriel is closing his cans of paint, cleaning his brushes, and moving what he can into the two-room shack. Each child is carrying something.

Lightning flashes across the darkening sky, blazes as it strikes the mountains to the north, the Santa Catalinas. There is a hush over the yard. Everyone gasps with every flash of fire and every roll of thunder. But they won't call the children in until the last moment, the moment that the rain comes down.

Lopez and Ignacio come hurrying across the vacant lot carrying five cans of paint, large cans, partly used. Nobody asks where they got it but Gabriel sees that one is red and he looks pleased.

They all stand outside waiting for the rain, Gabriel too because now it's too late for him to leave before the storm hits. Maria turns up her face, sniffing the air like any animal in the desert. Excitement moves through her body. The children too. They leap and run as the moment of the storm comes closer.

And when it comes there is no soft beginning. At once the rain pours heavily, furiously, so they are all wet by the time they reach the house.

There is an immediate new sound as the dry earth, the hard caliche soil gasps. You always hear it, a woman sound, as the earth sighs, sucks in the rain wherever it touches, pulls it deep down where the dry roots are. You always hear the desert when she finally breathes out, trembling and full. It's not the sound of rain; it's the sound of earth. Maria holds the door open just enough so they can all smell the rain. The children are standing on boxes at the window. It's suddenly dark inside, just the candlelight from the shrine.

They have brought in only the pot of frijoles from the outdoor wood stove — frijoles and the coffee pot. The coffee is lukewarm and there's just one cup but they pass it around. Anyone who wants a bite of the beans goes to the pot and lifts out a spoonful.

Manny doesn't get home until the rain has turned into a steady downpour, heavy and persistent, howling as it comes. He is drenched. He doesn't have any dry clothes in here but he takes off his muddy levis and blue work shirt and wraps a cotton blanket around himself and Maria thinks he looks fine that way. Fierce and beautiful without his white man's clothes. She still thinks of his belly, tries not to because it brought such bad luck this afternoon, but she can't help it. Her hands move as though they were there. Her hands feel that curve and she has to shake them to keep from reaching over to him now.

Rain drips through the roof, seeps under the front door, blows through the broken windows until everyone in the room is damp again. But the children curl up on the mattresses and some of them sleep, some of them answer every roar of the thunder.

In the darkness, talking softly, they tell Manny and Lopez and Ignacio about Mrs. Waterman coming to the house. Gabriel mimics her sharp English language sounds, so much harder than Papago words. "You got to plan ahead, you dumb Indian. You got to do this . . . do that. And no man around this house. No nothing . . . ."

Whatever children are still awake giggle as he speaks.

But Manny only nods. "You told her you got a plan?"

"I think so. I think I said I was going to get one."

"Aw, she was scared to say a word," Gabriel tells Manny. "You should of seen her."

The children laugh again.

Leaning against Manny in the darkness, Maria laughs too. *Now* she can.

"There is another thing," Maria says. "When I went to get the mattresses out of the yard one of them was gone. Somebody stole it. The tortilla pan too."

The children stop talking to listen.

"Those two things are easy to sell," Mrs. Domingo says. "You could go to any house and get a little something for them."

"Our daddy is back in town then," Anna says.

They all know it's true. Maria nods.

"I guess he didn't bring money back with him from California," Rose says. "I guess he had to have something for wine."

"He'll take whatever we have. Every day he'll take something to sell," Maria says.

"We'll put the padlock on this place," Mrs. Domingo says. "We'll just hand him food out the door."

"He gets mad for nothing," Jane says. "Our daddy. He hits for nothing. You have to run from him."

"He can't help it," Anna says.

Maria pictures her husband Jose Vasquez standing with the other winos against some building trying to keep out of the rain, pictures him with a pint wine bottle in his hands. Wonders who has her mattress now . . . her good heavy iron tortilla pan.

The rain slows, breathes, renews its force. They huddle there together, warm and close. Perhaps, after all, this is better than an overhang in the side of a cliff. Maybe they are a little dryer than their ancestors would have been.

CHAPTER 11

ST. JUDE

It is good to have a saint out in the fresh air, not always cooped up in a church. The Papago people like to be outside themselves; the desert is more their home than any house could ever be.

Besides, you need a saint here where you have your problems, not too far from the B-29 bar, not too far from the pool hall. From his cement and river-rock grotto Jude can see police shoving and kicking the winos into the paddy wagon, hears glass shatter as the bottles hit the street. He sees thieves and whores as well as old women in black mantillas.

Out on the reservation all the ancient shrines — not touched by white man's religion — are natural hillsides and rocks and crevices. A shrine can be wherever spirits let their power hover. Places where wind whistles out of the earth. Prayer feathers tied to thin green twigs. Rocks that hold magic. Shapes that are powerful. Out by Santa Rosa village, there's that circle of ocotillo stalks marking the Children's Shrine. It's dry, hot sandy desert now, but in this spot a spring of clear cold water once burst up from the sand to save the Papagos, dying of thirst.

Of course you don't expect that kind of magic from a saint in town. After all, he's not Elder Brother. But he's still a lot friendlier than cops or social workers. And another thing in his favor — he never says a cross word. What other white hands are pressed every day by so many dark ones?

Every now and then he does the kind of thing you'd expect of a saint on this street. Like keeping a drunk out of jail some night. Jude can make a quarter shine up from the gutter when you need it most, make it gleam like abalone shell in the moonlight, can make a poor wino's eyes focus on that quarter even though he can't see the cars in the road.

There are worse miracles than that. We thank you for such miracles, Jude.

CHAPTER 12

JOSE VASQUEZ

His good luck begins in the middle of the storm.

After a lifetime of bad luck who would guess that the turning point would come suddenly between flashes of lightning, between stomach pains, between belches, as he makes his way dizzily down the sidewalk squinting into a hard night rain.

"Jesus," he whines. "Awwww . . . Jesus."

Though the storm beats at him wildly, Jose Vasquez walks no faster than usual, maybe even slower than usual. He turns his face sideways, huddles down inside his dripping shirt.

He's dragging the thin double-bed mattress he just stole from the alley where Maria sleeps. And her old iron tortilla pan is inside his shirt. The rain strikes it with a heavy sound.

In front of the St. Jude shrine he hesitates. Maybe he should crouch back against the overhang for a minute, wait for the storm to pass, try to keep the mattress from being ruined. If it's too wet, nobody's going to pay for it. *Everybody's* got a wet mattress.

At that moment, lightning blazes. He sees something shining in the street . . . something. Leans the mattress up against the side of the shrine and goes back to look. The cement is slippery. He loses his balance and falls down in the water.

A quarter! Oh my God, a quarter!

He reaches out for it even before he tries to pull himself up. And there's something else there too, some kind of religious medal. He squints but he can't tell. There's a hole in the center. He's seen medals like that. Some kind of writing on it. Latin, he's almost certain. Latin.

He holds both prizes in his hands tenderly, warms them, dries them as well as he can, puts them into his wet pocket. But then he takes the medal out again — the good luck medal — and admires it.

Later he can look back on that moment, that flash of lightning when the good luck began. And though he is too drunk to remember exactly, he is sure the storm suddenly subsided and that rays of light spread across the sky the way it happens in movies when the crisis is past, when the lovers stand together at last on a hilltop in the wind. He even hears the music, mellow and rich, swelling, lifting. Ah, that moment out of all time. Just as it comes to Spencer Tracy, as it comes to Gary Cooper, it comes also to Jose Vasquez. Joe.

Another sign: a police car moving slowly down the wet street doesn't stop. For once, a police car passes by. Not even a glance toward the swaying wino, half-walking, half-kneeling, clinging to that mattress. Any other time that would have been it. He would have gone to jail. But tonight Jose Vasquez, a man with a good luck medal in his pocket, lifts his head to see that white car turn the corner and disappear. He sways toward the saint, moves his arm in the direction of the police car, and shrugs his shoulders in glorious disbelief. "Me," he grunts. Me . . . ." That's just the beginning.

Within an hour he sells the soggy mattress for two dollars. That's a good price, so good that it crosses his mind to take Maria's old tortilla pan back to her; she likes it so much. He doesn't, of course, but it makes him feel good that such a thought even came to him. It shows he's not so bad.

It's still raining when he gets to the B-29 bar and he knows he'd better hold his money in his hand or they won't let him in the door.

"Hey, Vasquez. You back?"

"Back from over there."

They aren't used to seeing him with two dollars in his hand. Drunk as he is, he senses their surprise. Tears fill his eyes. Tears of thanksgiving. Hope. Joy. He clasps his friends in the bar, embraces them, leans against them.

"Man, you seen your wife? She's living with a guy. That Manny. The one they say's so smart."

Jose shrugs. "Maybe he's rich. She'd leave me for a real rich man."

"No. They sleep out there in the alley. Just on a mattress there."

Jose turns his head sideways. It's the sly, knowing look he learned from the movies — those clever private eyes who pretend to believe the beautiful woman's story, but all the time they're setting the trap. That look. "Well, they sleep right down on the ground now," he says. "They got no double mattress no more."

"How come?"

He points his thumb toward his own chest and nods, shakes the two dollar bills in his hand, so they all understand and chuckle.

"The mattress, eh?"

"Yeah, who's so smart now?"

The mattress he sold is not the same one on which Jose and Maria used to lie together when he told her the stories of all those movies. He sold that one long ago for wine. Not for as much as two dollars though.

"Man, you bring a little money back from Yuma?" they ask. But they already know the answer.

He shakes his head. "What you think?"

They've all been on those field jobs, picking lettuce or melons or oranges or grapes. They know you never get home with a cent. After the boss takes out what you owe for beans and coffee and rice and for the cot they let you sleep on, then you're lucky if you get home at all. Especially the winos; they feel sick almost every day. Some days they can't move at all. It hurts too much.

Jose taps the tortilla pan under his damp shirt. "Got me something else to sell tomorrow," he tells his friends. Can't help showing off his good luck.

He unbuttons the one button on his shirt so they can see the pan. They nod. Everybody knows a good heavy tortilla pan will bring a dollar at any door on this side of town.

"That's money in the bank, that pan," one of them says.

"Well, at least I got her tortilla pan. Let her live with that rich guy. . . ." Himself—he's Tarzan, free and wild. They can have their pile of money.

"But that guy don't have no money," his friends remind Jose again. "He just chops cotton . . . like anybody. Goes to the dump sometime."

Jose's head is low against the table now and his eyes are almost closed, just slits in his dark puffy face.

"Let them live like white people if that's what they want. Not me." He tries to lift his head and can't.

Even so, he begins to tap the tortilla pan with his hand, harder and harder. Tarzan pounds his chest, his black iron tortilla pan chest.

"Rich bastard. . . ." But now he only mumbles. Can't talk any more. Almost out.

The bartender comes over and drags him up from the bench and shoves him out the back door. Jose and two others.

Any other night slumped down there in the alley, they'd be picked up by the cops, but Jose's good luck is a shield to them all. They sleep through the night undisturbed.

CHAPTER 13

Lupe Serra

Her belly is big but she isn't sure there's a baby in her. She's so full of magic, of voices, of owl cries. Sometimes snakes crawl slowly through the dark caves of her body. There's dirt in her too, damp black dirt, the kind geraniums like, a bucketful.

At that hospital when they noticed her belly getting large they only thought of a baby. White people don't know enough about magic to even guess at the things a *bruja* can put inside you.

Lupe comes on the bus from Phoenix two days before Mrs. Domingo gets the letter saying she is to be released. She walks from the bus station carrying her purple glass rosary and a comb and a typed letter and a bottle of pills in a paper sack. Whenever she comes to a street she waits five or ten minutes, sometimes longer.

She doesn't remember the way home, yet her feet take her there. She crosses that vacant lot with its greasewood bushes flowering yellow now from the summer rains, its tumbleweeds flopping down on loose stems, its prickly pear in fruit, a thousand thin new weeds among the broken wine bottles. Finally she sinks down under a familiar mesquite tree where the finches are singing in a tin cage.

Her own children run by and stop, surprised to see her there asleep on the ground.

"Mama?"

Mrs. Domingo comes outside. Rose too. Maria runs from across the alley and Gabriel from the other side of the house where he is painting the Papago-Apache battle on the wall. They look at Lupe, deep in sleep, her hands gently clasping her round belly.

"Hey, Lupe!" They wake her. Everybody kisses her, strokes her long tangled hair, pats her damp arms, holds her limp hands.

Lupe opens her eyes slowly, reaches out to touch her babies. Rose brings water, a plate of frijoles, a tortilla, but Lupe only drinks the water. Water to moisten the black earth in her belly. To keep it from making dust.

Nobody asks if she is better now because they all know white people's hospitals can't cure witchcraft. Why even ask?

Mrs. Domingo points out the St. Martin painting on the tin wall and the children run up and down the little paths lined with rocks shouting for Lupe to see how pretty the paths look.

"We sure been fixing this place up," Mrs. Domingo says.

"How come?" Lupe's voice is a whisper which they all bend toward.

"So we could keep your kids here. We had to."

Lupe shakes her head. "How come those little kids want to live so fancy?"

"Oh, not them," Mrs. Domingo says. "It was the welfare ladies didn't like it."

"They never even asked the children," Rose tells her sister.

But Lupe turns away and closes her eyes again. She doesn't like to hear people talking, even people she knows. The voices begin to tangle in her mind and she gets dizzy.

They let her sleep all afternoon and whenever she cries out or moans or gasps for breath it is her own husband, Ignacio, who makes the sign of the cross over her.

That first evening when they are all gathered outside watching the lightning over the Catalina Mountains, Mrs. Domingo asks Lupe the question she has been holding all day in her mind.

"You ran away from those white people, no? Even though they locked you in?"

Lupe chuckles, shaking her head. "I just fooled them so they let me go."

The children giggle.

"How?" everybody wants to know. "How'd you fool the white people?"

Lupe has her eyes closed again but Mrs. Domingo can't let her sleep yet.

"Tell how you got out of that place, Lupe. Stay awake and tell so we'll know what to say if they come around looking for you . . . trying to take you back."

Lupe slowly rubs her belly. "I just let them think I got a baby in me. They don't want you in their hospital if you happen to get a baby in you. They just tell you you're okay, go on home."

"But you do have a baby," Felipa, Rose's five-year-old, says. "Sure you do, Lupe." She points.

But Lupe shakes her head, shrugs.

Ignacio stares at his wife's belly but doesn't say anything. How would he know what that *bruja* can do?

"If not a baby, then what?" the children whisper.

Everybody wonders the same thing but it's Lupe's secret. She won't tell the things she feels in there. She doesn't want to sound crazy and get locked up again.

"Maybe this, maybe that," Lupe says. "Anyway, it's a good trick on the white people."

So the children laugh. They love tricks on white people.

Mrs. Domingo puts her stiff hands on Lupe's stomach but she can't tell. The other women too, Rose and Maria. They shake their heads. Everybody remembers certain stories.

146

"It could be a baby though," Rose says.

"Sure, it could," Mrs. Domingo agrees. "And that would be nice."

Lupe nods. She's tired, doesn't want to think about anything at all. She's using all her strength just trying to sit on the hot dusty ground and hold her body and mind together in one place. She doesn't know how long she'll be able to keep it up. She doesn't know how long she's been here now.

A week later a tall bony Anglo woman comes to the gate with an armful of papers. This time the children scatter. They know to go the other way whenever anyone except an Indian comes around. Especially if the person is carrying papers. Nothing good ever happens at an Indian house when an Anglo shows up with papers in his hand.

This one seems to have something to do with the hospital where Lupe was locked up.

"I'm sure we're all glad Mrs. Serra here has made such a fast recovery," she says.

They nod politely.

Mrs. Domingo points to the chair under the mesquite tree, doesn't want this woman to come into the house. You never can guess what they'll find to complain about. Anyway, it's cooler outside. Lupe has been lying in the shade. Now she sits up, pushes the hair back out of her face.

The visitor turns to Lupe. "Having a little nap?"

Lupe wants to act the way anybody else would act. She sits cross-legged looking down at the dry dirt, her hands on her belly. Whenever she hears voices she nods—yes, yes. When the white woman lifts her hands, her long thin fingers terrify Lupe. She looks away quickly. She doesn't want to scream.

Notice how that woman sits forward on the edge of her chair as though she wants to be ready to spring up. White people never know how to sit back relaxed in a rickety chair.

"Just a suggestion or two . . . ." This woman says. "Remember, I'm only paying a social visit to see how the patient is coming along. But I usually have a couple of good suggestions."

Nobody asks what those suggestions might be. Ignacio comes around the side of the house and stands leaning against the St. Martin wall, listening.

Finally the woman says, "Mrs. Serra is certainly looking . . . relaxed and comfortable."

Lupe continues staring down at the ground trying to keep her eyes open.

"And of course that's just wonderful . . . to be so relaxed. But you're probably wondering what you can all do to make Mrs. Serra feel even better."

No one responds.

"Well, here's one suggestion. Now we know that everybody needs to feel important. Right?"

Important? They look at that white woman as though she were the crazy one, not poor Lupe.

Important? The word hovers uneasily over the group. No one draws it to him, no one lets it settle, no one acknowledges its presence. They look at each other.

It's embarrassing really. Important is a white person's word. A Papago would hesitate to let anything so foolish come out of his mouth. Papagos make fun of a person who thinks he is smarter or cleverer than his brothers. They scorn one who puts himself forward. They smile behind their hands at Anglo politicians who say "Vote for Me, I'm best." A Papago couldn't get away with talking like that. Nobody would vote for him at all. Who'd vote for a man who was so conceited? If he has that fault, he will doubtless have others.

Papagos know that no man is more important than a deer or a spider or a stone or a cloud. All things are equal parts of the world and each one is needed to balance every other part. Just one 'important' person can throw the whole world out of balance, out of harmony.

Important? In the old days in council meetings no decision was ever made until all agreed. No white man's voting, no five against four, no eight against two. It had to be all. And things were done quietly, slowly.

Even now in school a white teacher can embarrass an Indian child by praising him too much. The kids know that's not the way the world is supposed to work.

No, white lady, just let each one fill his own space. What's this thing about being important? You keep that for yourself, eh? You're the one who likes it so much.

Now power, that's a different thing. But it's Indian power, spirit power, the kind that comes from visions and dreams and songs, from a good life, from blessings, from certain things the Indian people aren't telling . . . but never, never from a white man's job or white man's money. Never, never.

There can be long silences when an Anglo is trying to make Indians talk to her.

"Important," the white woman says again. This time her voice is louder. "Now you people don't have to look so surprised. There's no reason Mrs. Serra shouldn't feel important. How else is she going to have respect for herself . . . tell me that!"

No one tells her.

Lupe hears the words fighting in the air over her head and she knows she's going to have to hit them away with her hands if they don't stop soon. Even the soft sounds of Papago words can frighten her now and English words are so sharp they bruise her as they pass by.

"No, we're afraid Mrs. Serra wasn't made to feel very important here at home." She says it accusingly, looking first at Ignacio, then at Mrs. Domingo, then at Rose.

Ignacio goes behind the house for a sip of wine, comes back quickly, still running his tongue around his lips.

"So now maybe all together we can think of some things that you could do to help." She turns to Ignacio. "You too, Mr. Serra. We need a lot of good ideas."

"To make us feel important? Is that it?"

"Well, it's mostly Mrs. Serra we're talking about, of course. How can we make her feel important?"

Lupe raises her head and stares at them. The words have turned into flies and are buzzing wildly, sticking to her hair, her face. They are laying eggs on her. The air is black with them. She's breathing them, choking on them. She coughs, gasps, clutches her throat, spits.

The white woman turns back to Ignacio. "Well?"

"I got no good ideas," Ignacio says.

They know that soon enough she'll tell them what she has in mind. No use trying to guess.

She doesn't wait long. "Some people find that a part-time job can be very helpful. It gives the person — the patient — a change of scenery and a little pocket money too, and like I said, it makes her feel more important . . . ."

There is no response. Nothing.

"Well?"

"A part-time job. Is that it? You want her to find a part-time job?" Mrs. Domingo has to make sure she knows what expected of them.

Ignacio puts his hands to his eyes and squints toward the woman. Now he is watching her closely. "Listen," he says. "Lady, I could sure use that part-time job. What kind of job is it?"

She hesitates.

"Any kind of work would be okay," he says. "I don't care what."

She gets up from her chair.

"I didn't have a specific job in mind," she says. "You have to find your own job."

"Oh, well."

"Anyway, it was a suggestion for your wife."

"The thing is," Mrs. Domingo explains, "nobody around here's got a full-time job. And right now he don't even have a part-time job."

"Of course, I only counsel."

Before she goes, she takes out a white card with her name and phone number, looks around trying to decide who to hand it to, finally decides on Lupe herself. However, Lupe doesn't lift her hand to take the card so the woman puts it on the ground beside her.

"Bye . . . and you people feel perfectly free to call me any time."

"Oh sure. Thanks."

They sit quietly for a time. Lupe sleeps, thankful for the silence.

All of these Indians know the limp feeling that remains after white people have taken their words and gone back into their own world on the other side of town. Your blood doesn't flow again for awhile. You need sunlight and quiet and then finally someone will shake his head and stretch and slowly, slowly the breath will come back into you. At last somebody will laugh. This time it is Mrs. Domingo who chuckles. "Just be glad that lady didn't say old Lupe has to have a full-time job."

Sure, they agree. Be glad of that.

Ignacio doesn't have to hide his wine bottle now. He lifts it to his dry lips and then he says, "We got to give this thing a lot of thought. If they say she has to have a job, they mean it."

"But who's going to hire her?" Rose says what they are all thinking. "It's going to be real hard for her to get a job."

"It is," the children say. The way she sleeps on the ground all the time. Besides that, they remind Ignacio, she spits a lot and cries a lot and farts a lot. Who's going to hire her when nobody else can find a job either . . . .

"We'll think of something. We'll ask Manny."

Lupe raises her head and watches them. She knows only that something is warning her of danger. She may have to run. Even though she hasn't moved for an hour and her arms and legs are heavily pushing into the earth, almost rooted in that dry dirt, still she knows she may have to force herself up. Like any half-dead desert creature, too weary to move, she can call up hidden strengths when she must. Like a wounded rabbit lying in the shade of a weed, she can leap if she has too. But not yet. She waits, eyes closed.

The children stand looking down at her. "A part-time job," they say. "She has to get one. The lady said so."

"She has to be important too," Ignacio says. "Don't forget that."

CHAPTER 14

Maria Vasquez

You make it through the days to have the nights.

Nights. Guitar music and beer. That's when your kids flop down and sleep. Then you find whatever little bit of earth is quietest and darkest. Like any field mouse you choose your own circle of darkness and fit yourself to its shape, its space. You fit yourself to the man beside you and you fit yourself to whatever rocks you lie on.

By day you feel ugly and heavy and fat and shabby.

At night you feel the joy of your body, the perfectness of your size, the glorious fullness no skinny white woman's body could ever reach. You know yourself a circle, round as a melon, a sun, a seedpod bursting with seeds, whatever is complete. Large as a hill, you move when hills move, breathe when they breathe, slow and deep. You flow with oceans, you take your pleasure in the rise and fall of your great brown belly. Your laughter comes up from the center of the earth. Fat, fat with love, you hang on to Manny, swaying out over the world.

Since Jose stole Maria's mattress they sleep on the ground. Manny says he can find cardboard or maybe newspapers to put under their quilt but he never does. The truth is they both like the warm caliche soil under them and Maria sprinkles it and sweeps it every day to make it hard and even and clean. Let other people have the beds.

You spend your life walking the earth but you never really know it if you don't lie down on it. You have to touch it with the full length of your naked body night after night. Finally you feel its heartbeat as strong as you feel your own. You know its smell. And sometimes you'd swear you've sunk down into it during the night, down with all the roots, cozy as a nest. You can't believe it when you wake and find yourself lying up in the light with everybody else.

"We must be the tough ones," Maria says.

"We better be. It's our bad luck if we're not."

They have been asleep for hours when the dogs up and down the alley begin barking. Not the kind of barking that means fighting for a scrap of fat or whining an answer to some sad late-night serenade. It's the kind that jerks you up with fear.

Now they hear babies crying too, over by Mrs. Domingo's shack. Their voices carry the same kind of fear the dogs have. Manny and Maria pull on their clothes and run barefooted across the alley toward their friends.

"Shit," Manny says. "It's white men."

Two men stand at the door of the shack there by St. Martin shining flashlights across the yard, into the house, everywhere. Everybody knows at once who they are. Men from welfare. They always come in the middle of the night looking for a man. If a social worker suspects that a woman is taking a man into her bed at night, she'll send her spies to find out.

Only the babies are crying. The older children—some in the house, some out under the trees—just sit up in bed and suck in their breath and put their hands to their faces, but they do not cry out. They've already learned that. They watch; that's all.

"Mrs. Vasquez? Maria Vasquez?" the men are calling out at the door of the shack.

The door is open but there's no light inside.

"Maria Vasquez in there?"

The men with flashlights keep shouting into that dark silent room. "Special Services investigators for the county, Mrs. Vasquez. Mrs. Vasquez . . . ?"

Only dogs reply.

"They think you're in there. It's the address," Manny whispers.

Manny and Maria are still out of range of the flashlight beam. Maria clutches his arm.

"Then I got to go tell them that's me," she says. "Stay back. Don't you get caught."

There isn't any choice. Manny moves back into the darkness. Maria walks slowly to the door of the shack, faces the men alone.

As she stands there waiting for them to look at her, the door opens wider and Lupe looks out, Lupe, a tattered bathrobe pulled around her, her hair disheveled, her eyes blind with terror. Beside her, Ignacio, barefooted, his pants on now, no shirt.

"Maria Vasquez?"

Lupe nods. She wouldn't be sure about her name anymore. She just looks at them. Ignacio too.

Maria knows she has to speak. "I'm that one. I'm the one has this address. Maria Vasquez."

The men turn.

"No," one of them insists, "the one in the house is her."

They speak directly to Lupe. "That your husband?"

Ignacio says, "Sure, I'm her husband."

"Well, when she applied for welfare she claimed her husband was gone. Remember?"

"No, no," Maria says. "It's me. I'm Vasquez. They're Serra."

The men turn angrily to Maria. "You stay out of it. Let her answer."

The flashlight's darting eye probes that tiny room, flashes on the rumpled bed, the huddled children, the pile of clothes on the floor, the saints in their niche. The light goes back to Lupe still standing in the doorway.

"Now say your name."

But Lupe won't speak. Not a word. She stares at them.

"She's sick in her head," Ignacio says. "Excuse her."

Now the flashlight beam shines on Maria, moves up and down her body. She turns her face away until the light goes back to the ground. It shines on her bare feet.

"Okay. Your name?"

"Maria Vasquez."

"Your real name?"

"That's it."

"Then why weren't you in your house?"

"I . . . just went outside. I don't know why."

They look from her to Ignacio. "So who's the guy there in your house? Your boyfriend?"

Maria shakes her head, points to Lupe. "Her husband."

"Listen, you didn't just go outside. We been watching this place for an hour and nobody went in or out."

"I sleep outside," Maria says. "It's cooler out. I just like to sleep out."

Anglos don't know the pleasure of sleeping out. On their side of town right now there's probably not a soul sleeping in the yard.

"Sure," the man says. "These two just like to sleep inside and you just like to sleep outside."

"Yes."

"Okay, then where were you sleeping? In some guy's house down the road?"

Maria hesitates. Maybe they'll put her in jail for sleeping in a yard that doesn't belong to her. Finally she points across the alley. "There. I sleep out there with my kids. They like to sleep out too."

The white men look at each other, shine their lights across the alley. The beam passes across the yard where Carmen and Jane and Amelia are curled up together on a blanket and Errol Flynn lies with his head on a pillow, his body in the dirt.

The light swings up and down the alley, every side of the yard, catches Manny's leg as he is about to get into the abandoned car, moves up to his face. Without turning, Manny continues to step into the car, closes the door, leans back with his eyes closed.

"You got a very active neighborhood here," the Anglo says. "Who's the guy?"

"My cousin from Ventana," Maria says.

"He like to sleep out too?"

"He . . . ."

Maria's children are all awake now. They stand quietly in the darkness across the alley, don't run to their mother, don't make any sound when the light passes over them. One of the men takes out a notebook. "The names of the people occupying your house?"

"Serra. Lupe and Ignacio. And their children . . . let's see, the baby, that's Josefina, and then . . . ."

"Never mind the children. Just be so kind as to tell us why this Lupe person admitted she was Maria Vasquez."

Maria shakes her head. "She's a little bit crazy. She forgets her name."

"Oh, sure . . . sure. We all forget our names."

Maria does not reply.

The light goes back to Manny in the car. Now to the children. Now St. Martin. The light hovers over the saint and his pinto horse. "Boy!"

Without another word the men write in their notebooks, then turn and walk away. As they go they shine their lights up into the trees, to the tops of the shacks, the crumbling walls of the old adobe house, even the outhouse. However, they do not notice the swimming pool or all the people — Mrs. Domingo and Rose and Lopez and Rose's children — who have climbed the ladder and are watching them from the peepholes of the shelter that rises over the entrance to the pool.

Who can sleep now?

When the Anglos leave everybody gathers under the ramada. Ignacio brings out a kerosene lamp and they sit in its dim light whispering, touching. Even the children get up and come and sit leaning against each other. This is one of those times a house can't hold you as well as the open night.

They watch the stars. All except Lupe. She's walking now, a shadow that comes and goes without a sound. She stands apart from them, turning to look over her shoulder, that long bathrobe hanging loose around her big belly, her full heavy breasts. She carries Josefina with her wherever she goes.

"You know what," Mrs. Domingo warns Maria, "they'll cut off your money now."

"Just when we almost had us a house."

"Well, you never got the money yet anyway, so at least you won't miss it," Rose says. "At least you didn't get used to having it."

"Sure, that would have been a lot worse," Manny says.

Maybe. Maria knows today is no different from yesterday, the day before, a month ago. She isn't really any worse off now. It's only that she had begun to believe that since she had an address she must be close to getting a house after all. Still she knows — her mother used to warn her — it is not good to plan on things. It is always bad luck to expect good luck.

"Anyway," Maria says, "I'll be glad if that one, that social worker, doesn't hear about it for a day or two."

But Mrs. Waterman doesn't wait. She's there the next day before noon standing very straight, her face glowing with sweat, strands of damp hair clinging to her neck. She waits by the door glancing at St. Martin and the cowering beggar out of the corner of her eye, breathing heavily.

Nobody is around. No dogs, no children, no radio. The men are out of sight. Mrs. Domingo and Rose have taken the children across the alley to a neighbor's house so Maria can be alone if the social worker comes.

And what a time to be alone. She had clung to Manny this morning, something she had never before done in the daytime. Don't leave me. Let's run. Let's get a freight train together. What are we doing here anyway? My God. . . .

But she hadn't said a word.

Now she walks slowly toward Mrs. Waterman. Maria won't speak first. She waits.

"Well, Mrs. Vasquez, you certainly disappointed me." She takes off her sunglasses, shows her disappointed face.

Maria looks away. Does Mrs. Waterman notice she's a little bit disappointed herself?

"I thought we had discussed the rules about having a man in the house," Mrs. Waterman says.

Listen to those words. The English language makes words that come out of the mouth with such force, little grey rocks, sharp on one side. You could put somebody's eye out with words like that.

"You were observed, Mrs. Vasquez."

"Listen," Maria says, "couldn't those rules begin after I get the money, not before?"

Mrs. Waterman sighs. "Your poor children. That's all I've got to say."

"You mean because of not having that money?"

"Of course not. I mean being brought up with no moral values. When they see their own mother bring a man into the house . . . ."

"But what if I wasn't in the house?"

"Oh, my word, Mrs. Vasquez! The point is, we do not intend to use public money to support this kind of thing. And if you weren't the woman they saw in the house, the report says another man was seen with the woman outside."

"My cousin from the reservation."

"You sleep in the same bed with your cousin?"

"No, we just sleep down on the ground. We got to sleep somewhere."

She wonders if this is the day she'll go to jail. She could run the way Gabriel runs. It might be better than this. Another town. A different language even.

"There's no use my standing here if that's your attitude, Mrs. Vasquez. Now our investigators have made their report and if you want to file for a hearing that's entirely up to you. But you knew the regulations about having a man in that house. You knew."

God, Maria wants a beer. Thinks of opening her lips and tasting that first cool amber sip, hears Mrs. Waterman's voice flowing away, quieter and more distant as the beer goes down. There would be music too, good sad music getting louder as the voice gets fainter.

God, she wants a beer.

"Keep up this way and your children will be in foster homes, Mrs. Vasquez. Those children need proper training and proper surroundings."

"Okay, I'll get them."

Mrs. Waterman's face is dripping wet, pink from the heat, her dress sticking to her back. She turns to go, still talking as she walks away.

"You had every opportunity. All this office asked was that you provide a suitable home for those children . . . ."

Gone the beer and the music. Gone all hope of escape.

"I'll get it."

When that car drives away, the Indians return. The empty yard fills with people. Mrs. Domingo pours coffee and they sit on boxes and benches under the ramada and wait for Maria to tell them what happened.

"Was the white lady mad?" asks Amelia, her five year old.

Maria nods. "Real mad."

"Her voice is so loud," Rose says. "Way over there we could hear her fussing about a man in the house."

"White ladies make men stay outside," Amelia says. "They don't let them in."

After that white voice they need a little quiet. There are long pauses now.

Finally Mrs. Domingo asks, "How could you have a man in the house when you got no house?"

Maria shakes her head. "Yeah, but I couldn't tell her I don't have that house. Remember, I gave the address. To them, the address is the same as the house. They see no difference."

"I don't think it would have helped anyway," Manny says. "They say 'man in the house' but what they mean is 'man anywhere'. That's just what they call the rule."

"And that's the rule we broke," Maria says.

"You broke the 'man in the alley' rule," Anna says. "That one too."

Everybody smiles. At least they are by themselves now.

"Just get some other money instead of welfare money," Errol Flynn says. "Maybe we can still get a house."

Sure, everybody says. There are other ways to get a house without using their money. "Wait till I get my detective course done. I'll be making money. Plenty of it. Fifty a week easy."

"What lesson you on now?" Ignacio asks. "You find stamps to mail that last one?"

"I never found the stamps yet."

"You better hurry up," Mrs. Domingo says. "You doing good at it?"

"Like last time they gave us ten clues for a murder and I figured it out the first time. It was the guy that didn't leave his finger prints on the gun."

"How come?"

"He wiped them off."

"They all do that."

"Yeah, but he never thought of wiping them off of the bullets that were still in the gun."

"Dumb!"

Maria isn't going to let herself picture Manny bringing home money for a house. She keeps that thought from coming too close, keeps it a speck of light always just outside her line of vision. Any closer would be bad luck.

She still wants beer, a pitcher, one glass even. A beer first and then a freight train out of town. Men can do that. Why not women too? They make the women stay and face the Mrs. Watermans alone . . . .

"Mama?"

"Huh?"

"It's raining."

There are no more mattresses to run for now. Since Jose found that good luck medal in the street he can steal anything without getting caught. What kind of saint helps a man to steal? But that's the way with saints—if they like you they'll help you do anything. He got the kids' mattress last week so all that's left is the wood stove and a few plates and two pans and a couple of forks in the cardboard boxes. Anna and Errol Flynn run for the boxes and put them inside Mrs. Domingo's shack.

Maria sits under the ramada holding her coffee cup in both hands as the coffee gets cold and rain spatters against her face. It's still gentle.

"Come on, mama. Run."

"Not yet."

Let the rain touch her first. She turns to it, sucks it in like a weed. Her roots drink water. It takes awhile to get rid of the tightness in her body, to wash away the fear that clings to her. But rain has power, even a summer afternoon rain. That sacred water charges the body with life, renews. A woman or a corn plant—either one can be lifted up by rain. Suddenly the rain is hard and cold against her. Maria shivers. She takes a deep breath and turns to run toward the others in the shack.

It's that moment that Gabriel's voice lifts above the rain, shouting and laughing as he jumps the gate.

"Here comes Mr. Red Power, man. Re-e-e-e-ed Power!"

The children run out into the rain to meet him and Mrs. Domingo holds the door open. Following behind Gabriel are two young men who might be Indian—some kind of Indian—but even in the summer heat they are wearing suits and ties. White man clothes. How bad those clothes look on an Indian.

Gabriel gets to the door with a leap. Behind him the other two lower their heads as they run. They aren't laughing. Whatever kind of Indian they are, their spirits don't seem to soar in rain.

Everybody crowds into the tin shack. The children all want to stand beside Gabriel, to touch him.

Gabriel says, "Hey, meet some people who just got to town. Homer Lone Wolf and Raymond Clear."

The young men in suits put out their hands. Everybody shakes hands: Mrs. Domingo first, then Rose, Lopez, Ignacio, Maria, all the children. Everyone but Lupe. She won't let anyone touch her.

"They're Indian," Gabriel says. "And they're here to get a big Red Power thing going."

Homer Lone Wolf wipes the rain off his face with a white handkerchief and combs his hair before he is ready to talk. Then he says, "A meeting for your whole Indian community. Probably the most important meeting you people ever held here."

"We don't have too many meetings," Mrs. Domingo says. "The last one was for a tamale sale. Before that, a celebration for San Francisco's feast day . . . ."

"We'll turn this town on its tail," Raymond Clear says. Gabriel is smiling so the children smile too.

"No kidding," Homer Lone Wolf says, "you people out here in the sticks really need to be in touch with what's going on. You're still back in the Dark Ages."

Mrs. Domingo studies them very slowly, very carefully. "Where you Indians from?"

"Chicago."

She nods as though she had expected that exact answer. She turns to Maria and says, "Chicago."

Maria notices how like white people they seem, even their voices, so loud and certain. Louder than Indian voices. Are they really Indian? But of course Indians in other states may be different. So far away. Chicago. You couldn't expect them to act like Papagos or Pimas or Maricopas or even Apaches or Navajos or Hopis.

Manny would know what to think of them but Maria doesn't. Any Indian can put on white man clothes, sure. But these Indians talk like white men. Does that mean they think like white men too?

Gabriel is telling Mrs. Domingo, "They want to hold a big meeting."

"But not in any white man's hall," Homer Lone Eagle says. "It's got to be in an Indian place. Right?"

Nobody will say that it has to be in an Indian place. For a while there is silence.

Gabriel explains it. "That's what they do everyplace else. These guys know. They go around setting up meetings."

Ignacio says, "Not too many Indians got a big enough space for a meeting like that. Maybe outside . . . just a vacant lot."

But Gabriel looks at Mrs. Domingo. "I already told them about your swimming pool. That's a big place and we could borrow a lot of chairs. Everybody says that's the best place around."

Mrs. Domingo thinks it over. "Who's coming to this meeting?"

"All the Indians," Gabriel says. "All the young ones for sure and some of the old ones too. It's going to be the big thing."

"What's this meeting about?"

"Wow. You people are sure out of touch," Homer Lone Eagle says. "It's about Indian rights. Indian power. You want to keep on living this way forever?" He looks around the room.

Mrs. Domingo finally nods. "If everybody wants it I guess we have to share the swimming pool. It would be a good place for a meeting all right. But I only got two chairs. Remember that."

Raymond Clear tells her, "We'll take care of everything. There's a committee already planning it. We'll send somebody around with notices for all the Indian families just as soon as we set the time."

"Who'll carry those notices?" Mrs. Domingo asks.

"Anybody. Why?"

"Would you call it a part-time job, taking those notices around?" Mrs. Domingo looks at Homer Lone Wolf.

"I guess you could call it that. It isn't going to take more than a day or two anyway. Why?"

"Because I suggest my daughter, Lupe, for that job. She's supposed to get a part-time job and that would be it."

Homer Lone Wolf looks uneasily toward Lupe still huddled in the corner on the other side of the room.

"But there's no pay," Gabriel says. "We're all just trying to help. It's volunteer."

"She doesn't have to have pay," Mrs. Domingo says. "She just has to have a job. It's some kind of rule."

"For one day?" Homer Lone Wolf looks confused.

"One day would be fine," Mrs. Domingo says. "Then if anybody asks we can just say she had a job all right."

Thunder shakes the windows. Rain hammers the tin roof and trickles down onto the people inside the room. But every now and then the sun comes out. Crazy sun. Maria stands leaning against the window, watching. "You got you a house yet?" Gabriel asks her.

She shakes her head, doesn't want to talk about it in front of these strangers.

"Then you sure better come to the Red Power meeting. These guys can tell you what to do."

Homer Lone Wolf puts his arm across Maria's shoulder. "What's that? No house?"

Gabriel answers for her. "She sleeps out on the ground. Her and her kids. Cooks out there too."

Homer Lone Wolf's eyes flash. He makes a fist. "Good God, woman. And you just take it?"

Maria moves away and sticks her hands through the broken screen on the window, holds her fingers up to touch the rain.

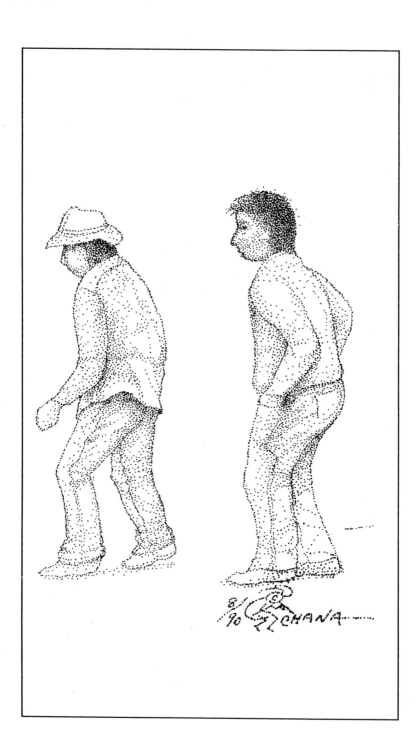

CHAPTER 15

JOSE VASQUEZ

Jose is getting used to good luck. He expects it now, is made taller by it, handsomer, fatter. His headaches aren't quite so bad and his teeth don't hurt so much. Even the pains in his stomach don't last as long when they hit.

Last week he saw a John Wayne movie three times. And now, for instance, this. The free dinner. Santa Maria, a free dinner! Just like that.

"You believe me now?" He chuckles as he reads the poster to his friend, Carlos:

FREE FREE FREE FREE FREE
DEMONSTRATION DINNER
LEARN TO COOK TASTY MEALS USING
YOUR FREE SURPLUS COMMODITIES

WHAT'S FOR DINNER?
Dilly carrots
Oriental Rice
Minced Beef Royale
Oatmeal Pudding

WHO IS WELCOME?
Everyone
(Bring your friends)
Monday, 2 P.M.
Community Service Hall
Sponsored by Eastside Women's Clubs United

"Dilly carrots," Jose repeats. "You had them?"

Carlos scratches his head. "Somewheres . . . ."

"Not too good?"

"Better 'n nothing."

White people aren't much as cooks but in this part of town you take what you can get. If there's a free meal you don't ask how it tastes.

Do Anglos really think all these Indian women have come to find out how to cook that free food? If they do they're crazy. There's not an Indian in town can't cook better than white people. Even the little kids cook better than white people. But everyone will listen politely just so the children can have full bellies for once. That's the price of the meal.

Jose holds the wall for support and squints at the poster. "Bring your friends. That's what she says, all right."

"Maybe we ought to go tell some of them guys over around the B-29. Maybe that Fuentes guy we passed lying on the ground."

"No, let's take it to them after. We can steal a lot of food in there."

Carlos shakes his head. "Yeah, but if the stuff's free, we just march in and grab it. We got as much right as anybody."

Jose grins. Sure. You forget you don't have to steal. Everybody welcome.

It's still too early for winos to try to get in. Jose knows that. Just because he's slouched over that way doesn't mean he isn't thinking, isn't sharp. Let the hall fill up first, then nobody will notice them.

Now if it were an Indian meeting with Indians running things it would be different. Indians have sense enough to know that the drunks get as hungry as anybody else. At least Indians will give you a place to stand back by the wall and they'll send the kids over with a plate of food.

But look at these white women. Every one of them glances over her shoulder two or three times while she's locking her car. Look how they hurry up to the door clutching their purses with both hands. All that just because two winos are squatting there in the shade of the building, their heads hanging loosely down, waiting for dinner.

The Indians have all heard about Jose's good luck and some of them come over to touch the holy medal. He keeps it in a small buckskin pouch tied with a string around his neck. Anybody can touch that pouch but he won't take the medal out. The way his hands shake, he'd worry about dropping it. He wants it close to his heartbeat, warmed by the sweat of his body.

He belches and his shoulders twitch as old Mrs. Domingo grasps that pouch with her stiff fingers, bends down to touch it to her lips, makes the sign of the cross.

"Okay, Joe. Thanks."

The children giggle because the whiskey smell is so strong, but they want to touch the magic too.

Jose even calls to Maria, "Come touch the good luck medal. Maybe you'll get some good luck out of it."

But she won't go close to him even though she doesn't have anything he can steal right now. He knows what she's thinking, all right. They both look at her shoes, flat black shoes from the Salvation Army store. Sure, they'll go some night when she's asleep. Somebody might pay a quarter for those shoes.

"No hard feelings," he says to Maria. "Go ahead. Everybody touches it." He is generous with his good luck, a holy man squatting there.

But Maria stands back. She just shakes her head.

"Don't say I never tried to do nothing to help that woman," Jose mumbles. "I said she could touch it. Even her. Even though she lives with another guy, I even try to do her a good turn. You saw me. No?"

"I did," Carlos agrees. "You sure tried to do them all a good turn. I saw that."

"You, Lupe," Jose calls out. "You need good luck. Come on."

Lupe is frightened at hearing her name. She jumps, wraps her arms tight around her body.

"Lupe's busy," Anna says. "She's supposed to be working. She has to have a job and this is it. Handing out papers."

Five or six children are gathered around Lupe, helping her, picking up the papers when she drops them, reminding her to hand one to everyone who passes by—Indians, not Anglos. The children say to people, "Take a paper. Take one of her papers," and then they have to hold up Lupe's hand.

"What's that paper about?" Jose Vasquez asks.

Lupe shakes her head.

"An Indian meeting," Amelia says.

"Don't you know about Red Power yet?" Anna asks him.

He knows. He's heard about it somewhere. "Sure I know."

The children guide Lupe over to him and she holds out a paper. He squints at the writing. "Yeah," he says. "Stop them Anglos stealing from Indians."

Carlos raises his head. "Joe?"

"Yeah?"

"You could go bless that meeting. Give it good luck. . . ." He sinks down again.

"You could," Anna says.

Jose folds the paper and puts it in his pocket. Why not? He has the power.

"Okay," he tells Anna. "They can count on me to be there. Where is that meeting at?"

"Down in the swimming pool," she says. "It tells about it on the paper. Everybody's going."

Joe. Jose Vasquez. He's needed now, needed by his people. He has something to offer. A wise man. A healer. Anyone who looks into his face ought to be able to tell. He feels himself Spencer Tracy, mellow and sad and knowing. He's a doctor who can save a life but nobody knows it yet; nobody gives him credit. He's the old Indian chief dying ill his tepee, whispering to his braves that there must be peace across the land. John Wayne at the Alamo. John Wayne wearing his hat . . . .

God, he'd like to steal himself a John Wayne hat. He'd pull it down low on his forehead. He wouldn't ask for anything else.

Most of the women are inside now but the children run in and out carrying the babies, following the ones who can walk, picking them up when they cry.

From time to time Jose calls out to the children, "They got the carrots and stuff done yet?"

"Not yet."

He's hungry, hasn't eaten since yesterday.

"Go look."

"The white ladies are still showing them how to fix everything. They're making the people who get the welfare food write down how to cook it."

If they don't hurry he's going to be too dizzy to make it to the door. "Now?"

The children peer in the door. "They've got a lot of pictures up. They're showing what food is good for you."

"We going to skip them pictures."

Us too, the kids agree.

Finally it is time. Anna has come out to motion to them. "You better wipe the spit off your mouth," she says.

Both men move their arms slowly across their faces. They have some trouble getting up, focusing their eyes on the door. Jose, the man with the saint's blessing forever with him, goes first. Let Carlos follow behind. John Wayne leads the way.

"You got nothing to worry about," he says.

But when Jose stands in line with his plate in his hands the white women stop smiling and begin to whisper to each other. Their eyes are on him as they whisper.

Jose's head flops now and then but he is careful to stand as straight as he can. He is hardly swaying at all. He feels the saint's hands holding him up, touching his ribs, pushing very slowly along.

Three of the white women group together at the serving table.

"Sir?"

Jose tilts his head back so he can see them. Very dressed-up ladies. Pearl necklaces. Shiny earrings. Stuff you could sell anywhere. You could live a month on that money. A year maybe. Your whole lifetime. You could buy a John Wayne hat. You'd get wine by the gallon, not the pint.

"Pardon me, sir, but . . . ."

He doesn't realize at first they have been speaking to him. He grunts, holds out his plate.

The woman with the serving spoon in her hand says, "This little meeting of ours is really just for the ladies in the neighborhood, so I think it would be better for you . . . ."

"Easy on the peas," he says, though no one is serving him anything at all.

"It would be better for you to leave. I'm sure you understand." She turns the corners of her mouth up, quickly lets them down again.

"Huh?"

"In the afternoon like this, of course we thought the men would be at work . . . ." It's another one of those Anglo women. She speaks even faster than the first one.

Jose Vasquez squints at her. "Everybody welcome."

And Carlos says, "Me and my friend work late. Nights. That's how come we're off now."

"We got time to eat," Jose says.

Carlos picks up a plate too, holds it out.

The women whisper again, stepping back from the table. Then they march forward.

One of them says, "I'm sorry. Another time maybe."

Nobody moves along the line.

"Easy on the peas," Joe says again. He lets his head roll down but the saint's gentle hands help him lift it back into place. At least he keeps holding the plate straight out in front of him.

If this had happened a month ago he might have given up, but now he trusts his good luck. He's willing to wait if he has to. A saint can't always work things out in a second. You have to give him time.

"Sir!"

He stands there holding his plate. So does Carlos. It's very quiet in the room.

But how can a few Anglo women withstand the force of a saint? They can't. They have to give up. After two or three minutes the one who is serving mumbles, "Oh, for heaven's sake," and sighs and spoons out the food. The serving spoon hits the plate angrily.

Across the room Lupe begins to moan. It's the kind of wailing you hear sometimes at night when you can't be certain whether it's human or not. That kind of deep insistent cry. Now the sounds gather into a word.

"No . . . no . . . no."

They have been trying to persuade her to taste the food but she pushes the spoon away and covers her mouth with her hands.

"Just one bite," Rose begs her. "You need food. You do. And it's free."

"It's poison," Lupe whispers. "I won't eat poison."

"It isn't poison," all the children try to tell her but Lupe is ready to run.

"Don't make me eat poison." Her voice is louder now.

"I bet it's them dilly carrots," Carlos says. "They're not too good."

Jose moves slowly across the room to Lupe. "Here, I'll eat it for you. Just to show you it's okay. I'll take that chance on myself."

A hero, he offers himself. Everybody watches. He hands his own plate to Carlos to hold, takes Lupe's plate. She has dropped her fork but it doesn't matter. He pushes the food into his mouth with his fingers. Gulps. Chews. Chews. Swallows. Gulps. Belches.

"Not poison," he tells her. "See. I didn't die."

"It takes time," Lupe says. "It could be later."

Jose takes his own plate back from Carlos. "I got good luck. It won't kill me."

The white women gather behind the serving table now, all of them together. They aren't trying to smile anymore. Their whispers rise sharply over the room. They light cigarettes and nibble tiny bites of food and keep looking out the window. Finally a man arrives carrying a camera and all the women go over to meet him. As they talk to him they keep watching the Indians very quietly eating their free meal.

Now one of the women walks rapidly to the microphone which stands on the platform where the large color pictures of wholesome foods have been arranged. Her high heels click as she walks.

"Ladies . . . if I may have your attention. There's a photographer from the newspaper here and he'd like to take a picture of some people who are enjoying the nice meal that we worked so hard to prepare for you."

Her voice shakes.

Another of the white women comes to her side and says into the mike, "How about some of the children . . . those little girls there in the corner? I think they are enjoying their dinner."

People stand back to watch. The white women keep telling the children to smile when they taste the oatmeal pudding. The children nod but when the women bend dowm to have their picture taken handing pudding to the Indian children, the women are the only ones smiling.

Now the whole group of Anglo women demonstrates smiling. They show their teeth and say, "Look—like this . . . ."

"Can we get a kid over here who knows how to smile?" the photographer asks.

Jose has been watching the picture taking but now he signals to Carlos and goes back to the long serving table and picks up all the dishes he can stack, ten or twelve, and stuffs a handful of forks into his pocket and walks slowly to the door as the flashbulbs blaze on the other side of the room.

At the door he puts the plates down and comes back inside for the pan with the rice in it. St. Jude be praised, there's still plenty of rice there. Oriental rice.

Outside Carlos picks up the plates and they move slowly down the street in the bright afternoon sunlight, swaying slightly as they glide along.

"I wonder was the oatmeal pudding any good," Carlos says. "We missed it."

"Aw, I didn't like the people enough to hang around there. They didn't seem too friendly."

Out in the dusty alley behind the B-29 bar they set the pan of Oriental rice and the plates down on the ground. Anyone who passes by gets to help himself. There aren't enough plates but it doesn't matter. People just dip out of the pan.

After a while Jose reaches into his shirt front, draws out a pair of sunglasses, five spoons, two ballpoint pens and an unopened pack of Kool cigarettes. Besides all that, the forks in his pocket.

His friends whistle softly between their teeth. "Man, you swipe it all at one place?"

He shrugs modestly. "Have a smoke. Go ahead, my friends. On me."

The Kools are passed around. Everybody lights one and puts another in his shirt pocket.

"They didn't serve no wine, huh?"

Everybody grins. They move to the shade, leaning back against the adobe wall of the bar, their bellies full of Oriental rice, slowly dragging on their king-size cigarettes.

If he had a John Wayne hat now, Jose Vasquez would pull it down low on his forehead. He'd let that hat keep the rest of the world out of sight. He'd close his eyes under that hat. Under that hat he'd be a new man.

He sleeps standing up.

CHAPTER 16

GABRIEL SOTO

He looks up and she's poking her head around the corner of the tin shack smiling at him and holding out her bottle of Coke. He's not dumb. Knows what she's offering is her cool, hard suntanned body. He takes the Coke, puts his lips where hers have been, gulps it down.

"Flaming Arrow, that picture! It makes my heart pound just looking at it."

She touches her heart. "Really."

Gabriel nods. "It turned out pretty good."

That battle is suddenly the background for their lives, not the tin shack it is painted on, not the alley, not the mesquite tree. An overwhelming presence, that battle. A reality. They move in its force, could be swept away any second. Could get an arrow in the gut. She could die. He'd have to save her.

Sue Mills can only whisper. She lets her fingers brush his arm as she points. "The Papagos winning?"

"Sure they are. Eleven Apaches are dead, see. Only three Papagos."

"God," she whispers.

Together they watch that bloody fight. Hiding close together in some high rock crevice, they peer down onto the wide desert battleground where beautiful bare brown men use spears and bows and arrows. They watch them darting behind sahuaros, kicking up dust. They see the buckskin fringe and eagle feathers on the shields move in the wind as the warriors run. And high overhead hawks float . . . .

"That's the way it used to be," he says.

"You'd have been there fighting too," she says.

Today he isn't running from her. An Indian afraid of a little runt of a social worker?

"That's my heritage," he says. "I'm just like them. My blood's the same."

"I know that." She looks into his dark face. "Listen, I'm not a case worker today."

"They fire you?"

"No. I mean I'm not here on business for Mrs. Domingo or anybody. I just came to tell you something."

He's on guard now but his hands never stop moving slowly up and down the Coke bottle.

"Remember when you were painting the saint there on the other side? Well, I kept thinking about it . . . ."

She lets her hair flow and ripple as she moves. Gabriel still isn't sure whether she's dancing or just stretching. Even her fingers turn and bend. Flower petals, those fingers. Any breeze could move them.

"You must have thought I was really stupid not to see the symbolism in your painting. I mean, it was so clear. So symbolic of the struggle!"

"That St. Martin picture?"

"But in a way I'm glad you didn't tell me. You were sort of testing me, weren't you? Weren't you, Flaming Arrow?"

What the hell is she talking about? He turns up the Coke bottle even though there isn't anything in it.

"Maybe I was . . . and maybe I wasn't."

"Not that I blame you for testing me. You had to. But it came to me in bed that night. Like . . . cutting the garment in two pieces. That's obviously the split between the two cultures, Indian and white. Right?"

He looks at her, finally grins and nods. "You sure got that one."

She claps her hands. "I knew it. And the beggar's rejection of it. That's the Indians' rejection of half a loaf. It was suddenly so clear."

Of course Gabriel knows that the beggar isn't saying no to that half a cloak, but he can see that it might look that way. Maybe the old guy should have said no.

"It was as if I was meant to understand it," she says. "Sort of a . . . don't laugh at me . . . ."

He isn't about to laugh. Actually, he's numb. Her voice is coming at him from all sides, enclosing him, hitting him gently everywhere at once, pouring like warm water over his fingertips, his balls, his toes.

"Sort of a miracle. Like I was really meant to understand you."

"Man, you are crazy!"

That look on her face. That's the way the books about the saints always show young girls who've just seen a vision of the Virgin of Guadalupe. Come to think of it, that's the way they show Guadalupe too.

"It just came to me," Sue repeats.

Gabriel shakes his head. He'll accept that miracle all right.

She puts her scarf on the ground and curls up on it and leans back against the tin shack.

Every time she moves her legs he can see the bright blue panties under her short skirt. So shiny and new looking, not the faded sagging things girls around here wear, elastic worn out, somebody's old stained giveaway . . . if they wear any at all.

"You can't believe it, can you?"

"Believe what?"

"That a non-Indian like me can be so attuned to your thoughts?"

He shrugs. He's still cool, one of the coolest guys in the world. Pulls his headband lower on his dark straight forehead. Just for the hell of it, takes off his shirt and ties it around his waist.

He's glad he told her his name was Flaming Arrow. That's what it should have always been. Now as he finishes up the painting, he's Flaming Arrow for sure. He's naked and he's got an eagle feather in his headband and turquoise chunks hanging around his neck. He's out there by Baboquivari Mountain and it's at least a hundred years ago.

Suddenly like any coyote alone on his dry rocky ledge, he raises his head and sings out. Loud. Doesn't care who hears. Doesn't care if he wakes up some drunk.

The song comes out in words he didn't even know were in his mouth. . . .

> *Heya, heya*
> *Oh he oh*
> *Oh he oh*
> *Heya he he*
> *Oh he oh*

Sue sways from side to side, her eyes closed, sways to the rhythm he beats on the bottom of a five pound Folgers coffee can which still has a little red paint in it.

Now of course Anna and Errol Flynn and Josefina and Carmen and maybe three or four other kids come flying around the side of the house. They stop when they see the social worker but she opens her eyes and stops swaying and gets up and hugs them.

"Hi, lovey," she says to each one.

The children are carrying armfuls of papers, notices for the Red Power meeting.

"We got to go with Lupe to hand them out," Anna says. "If we don't, she gives them all to St. Jude. He's already got about a hundred papers."

"Oh, what's that?" Sue asks.

But the children hold the papers tight against their bodies. They've been told to give them to Indians only.

"It's okay," Gabriel says. "Give her one."

She gasps with delight when she reads it. Her eyes go back to Gabriel.

"I knew you'd be in on this. I knew it! Right at the heart of the struggle!"

"Yeah."

"And I want to help too. Any way I can." Her voice is small but intense.

"Can she?" the children ask. "Even though she's not an Indian can she come to the meeting?"

"Oh, please," she begs, moving closer to Gabriel.

"You might be able to. I got to think about it."

She reads every word of the notice now, exclaims over it. "In the swimming pool! What a fantastic place for a meeting."

"It was my idea," Gabriel admits. "Some guys came to town to set up the meeting but they didn't know where to have it. They wanted it to be a place that didn't belong to Anglos, just to Indians."

The children all watch Sue Mills. They've already learned to hold their own thoughts far back behind their round secret faces. But this golden social worker isn't like them, isn't like Gabriel. She flings her thoughts out to the world and lets them fill the sky like colored balloons.

"I'm so excited for you, Flaming Arrow," she says. "It must be marvelous to know you're helping your people."

"That's why I was in a hurry to get this picture done. Because it's a real Indian kind of thing."

"Sure," Anna says. "Everybody will look at it on the way to the swimming pool."

Mrs. Domingo comes toward them leading Lupe down the path. Lupe's belly is a separate burden looming in front of her. She holds it with both hands as she walks, slowly, wearily. With every step she sways. The children help to hold her up.

"Just give out a few papers and then bring her back," Mrs. Domingo tells the children. "She might have that baby any time."

"If it *is* a baby," the children remind her. "*If*. . . ."

"It's pretty heavy to be a baby," Anna says. "It might be something made out of iron."

But then they remember not to speak of such things in front of an Anglo. They whisper to each other. Rocks. Maybe it's rocks . . . .

Lupe and the children pass through the gate single file, all of them reflecting that heaviness.

"Flaming Arrow, could I ask . . . ?"

But he isn't about to start explaining that heavy belly to this Anglo girl. She might figure out the symbolism of old St. Martin's red cloak, but she'd never understand how some *bruja* managed to put a bunch of rocks in Lupe's belly. All the little kids understand it but this girl wouldn't. They didn't teach that in the course she took.

Mrs. Domingo brings out coffee. She looks at the battle scene as she passes by on her way to the washtub under the tree.

"Last time I looked, I counted ten dead Apaches. Now looks like another one dropped down."

"Apaches don't fight as good as Papagos. I told you."

"For once," Mrs. Domingo says, "I wish your grandfather out at Baboquivari could of seen that picture. He was scared to death of Apaches all his life."

Gabriel knows she isn't joking but Sue thinks she is so she laughs.

But suddenly the laughter stops. She raises her hands to her face. A look of true revelation passes over her again. Either she's making a habit of seeing old Guadalupe or . .

"Oh, listen," she says, holding up the Red Power notice. "Something just came to me when she was counting up those dead Apaches."

"What came to you?"

"Well, thinking of the meeting, you know. Honestly, shouldn't you be showing your ancestors fighting off the white man, the invading white man who is stealing the land — not another Indian tribe. Don't you see, the Indians are all brothers. It's the white man they should fight."

Gabriel does see. "I got to admit it. Red Power is Indians together against Anglos. That's true."

"And when they come and see this picture of two tribes fighting so wildly, well, it's just not in the spirit of the meeting."

Mrs. Domingo faces Gabriel. "Wait a minute. Nobody told me we were going to fight the whites down there in my swimming pool."

"No," Gabriel says. "Whites aren't even coming. It's an Indian meeting."

"The point is," Sue explains, "that Indians have to band together to accomplish anything."

"I could paint all around those walls down there in the swimming pool," Gabriel says. "A battle of Papagos against Anglos. Man, what a fight. Every side of that pool."

Sue touches his arm.

Mrs. Domingo has started over to the washtub but she turns around and comes back. "Hang on. There's just one thing you two Indians forgot."

Gabriel won't ask her what it is. Let her keep it to herself.

But she tells them anyway. "You forgot the Papagos never fought the white man. They were peaceful people. Farmers. Gathered a little cactus and planted their corn and melons and beans there in the washes. They never cared much for fighting. To tell the truth, they never lifted a hand against the white man."

"Come on! Sure they fought. All the tribes fought."

Mrs. Domingo shakes her head. "Go ask your grandma. Ask any of the old people. They'll tell you the same thing."

Sue Mills says, "Well, they fought symbolically at least. That's what we're talking about."

Mrs. Domingo only smiles. "Oh, well then. I sure thought you were talking about the Papagos and the whites. And I'm saying *they* didn't fight."

"Well, they're going to fight now. All around that wall."

The old lady goes back to the washtub under the tree. Gabriel is glad she's not going to argue about it.

"Will she mind?" Sue asks him. "After all, it's her swimming pool. What if she doesn't want that kind of painting?"

"She don't care. She likes any pictures."

So Gabriel and Sue walk toward the swimming pool.

"Just to see where you'll be painting," she says. "Just to get the feeling of it."

Gabriel Soto—Indian artist—Flaming Arrow, is calling forth the truths and insights and mysteries of his fierce ancestral past. He's caught up in the spirit of the dream and he knows it's her dream too. You can see that by the look in her eyes as she walks beside him across the yard.

Crazy, crazy, he thinks . . . the way she reaches into his thoughts. Like that thing of St. Martin and the coat. It was sort of in his mind as he painted it. He remembers that now.

They're almost running, hurrying toward the splintery little door that leads into the pool. They crawl backward down the steps and enter the dark sunken room with a jump, the way you'd fly into a pool with water in it. They want to spring, to move. Her arms rise, lifting like wings.

They look at those blue swimming pool walls as though they were already covered with paintings. Marvelous paintings.

"Oh, hurry, hurry," she says.

He moves close to her.

"I am."

"You'll have to paint every second to get it done in time. But I'll . . . I'll be with you."

She is dedicating herself. A sacrifice. An altar. He touches her face and she begins shaking and gasping very gently. This has become a holy time, a ceremony. An ancient ritual.

"Take off them blue pants," he says.

She does. She holds onto him with one hand and pulls them off with the other and throws them on the floor.

It's very dim down here, dim and quiet. Just one chicken wandering around pecking at splinters of sunlight that come down through the roof.

"Flaming Arrow, aren't you going to undress? We have to be completely free with each other. We have to see each other."

She unbuttons her dress, steps out of it, lets it fall, kicks off her sandals. He begins to pull off his boots, hopes to God those kids stay out of here.

"There's no way to lock the door," he says.

"I'm not ashamed, Flaming Arrow. I'm proud. I don't care who knows."

She's lying down now, her head flowing downwards with the slant of the pool, naked, waiting for him. So it looks like the good luck time of his life is finally beginning, he thinks. Not many people around here would have bet that Gabriel Soto would be fucking a blonde social worker this week.

"I knew it from the first," she whispers as his hands move across her small breasts, circling the tiny hard nipples he's been watching under her dress. "Didn't you?"

"Not me. I only just found out."

Even though she's shivering she keeps talking. "Everything must be very basic and simple . . . and tribal and pure between us, Flaming Arrow."

"Okay."

"Do anything you want to me."

Her eyes close as she says it. This is so *sacred*. Not like rolling onto any other girl. Gabriel feels like he is about to dishonor the Virgin of Guadalupe. Her smiling face is raised to him. He might as well be drunk. Isn't sure he's going to land on her when he falls. But he does. Goes into her immediately and is startled to hear her scream out loud and long and clear, "Flaming Arrow. Oh my God!"

The chicken, even more startled than Gabriel, squawks and flaps frantically to the other side of the pool.

They're going to hear this white girl a mile away, he thinks. But now she's the Virgin of Guadalupe again. She raises herself up, stiff as a saint, falls back twitching.

"You're just the most beautiful wild Indian brave," she whispers. "I'm glad you left your headband on."

He cradles her in his arms, turning her so he can see the suntan lines. Feels her smooth white ass, just can't believe it.

"Flaming Arrow, I'm dedicating myself to the Indian cause — I'm part of your struggle . . . ."

"I can see that you're sincere, all right."

"I *am*. Go ahead, Flaming Arrow. Tell me whatever is in your heart. Be frank with me. Don't think of me as a white person. Think of me as another Indian."

"I'm trying to," he says.

"I know it's hard for you to verbalize in English. So if you want to, just go ahead and speak to me in your native language. I'll know what you're saying even if I don't know the exact words. Really, I will. I'm that sensitive to you."

He can't tell her how little Papago he knows but he tries out a few words on her, not really full sentences. As he speaks her hands move across his body.

"I got to admit what you said, Sue. You do seem to know what I'm thinking."

She clings to him, pushes against him. Finally breathes and relaxes, sinks down.

"I came again," she says. "Just because you said that."

He is stricken at the power of his words. "Jesus!"

"That shows the spiritual quality of our relationship."

He agrees, it does.

She starts to get dressed, then stops. "I wish we could go naked, really be free and natural in the Indian way. You must hate to have to wear clothes. It must seem so false to you."

"Yeah."

"Well, it does to me too."

He lights a cigarette and they lie on their backs looking at the blank blue walls on which the Papagos will battle the invading Anglos.

"Honestly, Flaming Arrow, I think you can teach me to be as primitive as you are."

"I think I can," he says. "It may take awhile, but I'm willing to try all right."

They roll down the slanting pool floor and the chicken runs to get out of their way and up above them the children are calling that there is somebody who wants to talk to Gabriel about the meeting. The Red Power meeting.

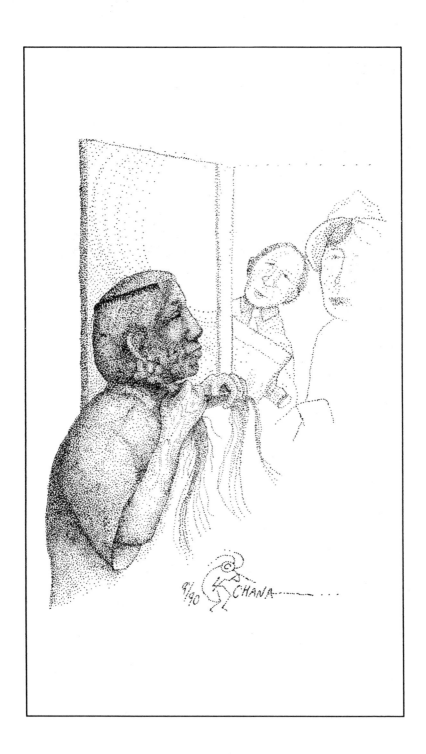

CHAPTER 17

MRS. DOMINGO

The first people at the Red Power meeting are white people. They stand at the open door of Mrs. Domingo's shack. Still braiding her hair, she peers out at the two men, one with a notebook in his hand, one with a camera.

"We're looking for a meeting somewhere around here. Some kind of Indian meeting."

"This is it."

She's surprised. Didn't know they were going to let whites in. Thought it was supposed to be just for Indians.

"Here?" One of them has the printed notice of the Red Power meeting in his hand.

"Well, not *right* here," she says. "Over in the swimming pool."

"Yeah?" He looks around doubtfully and laughs. "We supposed to wear swimming suits?"

Mrs. Domingo doesn't answer him.

The one with the camera glances at his watch. "They told us three o'clock."

Mrs. Domingo sticks her head farther out the door to see the sun. "That's right. About then."

"But it's past three now. You sure they're having a meeting?"

She shrugs, goes back inside and closes the door. Lupe is asleep and Mrs. Domingo wants to get her up for the meeting. She brings a damp rag to wash her face, to cool her throat.

Lupe opens her eyes, moves her hands across the great rise of her belly, a mountain weighing her down.

"Come on, Lupe. You better go with us to that meeting."

Lupe shakes her head no.

"They say everybody's going to get a lot of good out of this thing. Those smart Chicago Indians are going to tell everybody what to do. Just tell them your problem."

"No," Lupe says. "No."

Mrs. Domingo wishes Rose could be here too because she always enjoys meetings. Too bad she's in jail.

The men are at the door again. They knock with the sharp hard sounds Anglos make at Indian doors. An Indian couldn't make that sound.

"It's way past three. Any suggestions?"

"It could be some other day. Maybe you better not wait."

They wait anyway, standing by the St. Martin painting. What's the matter with them, Mrs. Domingo wonders. Didn't they ever see a saint before? Look how they stare.

It's another half an hour before the first Indians begin walking slowly down the alley. Even though it's almost four o'clock, they pause in the shade of the mesquite tree before going on toward the swimming pool. They have time to stop. From her door, Mrs. Domingo watches her friends arrive. In any Papago group, the movements are slow and the voices quiet and there is laughter. But Indian laughter always sounds different from Anglo laughter. It comes from a different direction, she thinks, maybe up from the feet, not out of the top of the teeth like the laughter of white people. The Indian way, it becomes accustomed to the body before it leaves it.

Lupe is on her feet now, moaning and swaying as the children move her along the path to the pool. Jesus Gomez, the Ramada Builder, is with them because he feels at ease with the children. And the winos walk along with them too.

Jose Vasquez and his friends like the slow pace and they like the company too. They don't have to talk to each other unless they want to, but they keep telling Lupe it's going to be some important meeting down there. A big Indian meeting.

The only people moving fast are those two Chicago Indians, Raymond Clear and Homer Lone Wolf. They're making the rounds shaking hands with everybody. The young Papagos walk with them, the ones in headbands, the cool ones, the ones who carry books and papers and pencils, the ones who wear beaded necklaces.

Mrs. Domingo feels a stir of excitement. Maybe the young ones are right. Maybe the Chicago Indians came to save them after all. She squints in their direction and shakes her head.

So many people are here. It's almost a fiesta, some kind of good summer fiesta. The swimming pool is decorated with pink and yellow paper flowers and there are new candles in front of the San Francisco shrine. Somebody has even cut a hole in the roof so a light bulb can dangle down from the long string of extension cords that snake along the ground all the way across the alley from Mrs. Fuentes' house.

Boards have been set up on packing crates to hold the food — bowls of frijoles and chile and roasted corn still in the husks, fresh flour tortillas stacked up and covered with dish towels. Everybody brings something and puts it down and stands back and admires the table.

But the smell of fresh paint overpowers even the good strong smell of chile. People have to be told not to touch the walls of the pool where Gabriel's painted Indians, bare and tall, dark hair blowing in the wind, charge an army of scowling fat whites. It's bows and arrows against rifles. It's eagle feather shields against boots and hats and mustaches and pale yellowish eyes. Look how the sacred eagles fly over the Indians. Only rattlesnakes and scorpions stay with the whites. You see them by every rock.

Everybody who comes to the meeting looks at that battle, follows it around the pool. That's very pretty, people say. Man, that's a fine picture. Look how those Papagos fight!

It takes a long time for the old people to make it down the steps into the pool. They go slowly, holding on to their grandchildren for support. Some of them take five or ten minutes to walk those six blue steps and reach the slanting cement floor. They don't mind the slant; that's like walking a hill. But they aren't used to many stairs. By the time they get down, they're chuckling and shaking their heads as though they had been caught doing something ridiculous. The crazy things you get yourself into when you live in town. Crazy white man things!

Mrs. Domingo stands back, watching. It's her swimming pool, all right, but it's not her meeting. She and her friend, Mrs. Reyes, find seats on the last row.

It is a good feeling to see your friends gathering. If the Indians from Chicago just won't talk too long, everything will be fine. They can have their potluck dinner and be at ease and hear Papago voices around them. The swimming pool seems suddenly like a feast house out on the reservation.

Raymond Clear and Homer Lone Wolf have chairs facing the people. The reporters are both following Sue Mills around the room as she points out the tribal symbolism hidden in the details of Gabriel's painting.

Finally one of the young Papagos stands up and says, "Okay, I guess this meeting is starting."

"Talk Indian," somebody calls out. An old woman.

"I guess you're right, Mrs. Villa. Maybe somebody . . . you, Mr. Juan . . . come on up here and do the whole thing in Papago."

But Raymond Clear stands up. "Now wait a minute. We don't speak Papago. The meeting's got to be in English."

"Some Indian meeting," one of the old people mutters.

Mrs. Domingo and Mrs. Reyes exchange glances. Mrs. Domingo would like to ask the Chicago Indians if they speak any Indian language at all. She can't imagine Indian words coming out of their mouths.

But the young Indians defend Raymond Clear. "Listen, these guys are here to help us. They're not going to be much help if they don't know what we're saying."

Raymond Clear and Homer Lone Wolf nod. "Right!"

Still the old people sigh. They look at each other, not at the young ones.

Sue Mills comes to the front table. Her long blonde hair is braided today, a feather tied to the end of each braid. She touches Gabriel as she passes.

"How about this? Somebody can translate into Indian. Then everybody understands. I personally feel it's very, very important for these people to use their own language."

"Sure it is," Raymond Clear agrees.

So that's it. Translating makes everything take a long time but the old people don't mind. The man who is translating speaks very slowly and smiles when he is speaking and puts in a number of good Papago jokes. Almost none of the young people, the town kids, speak Papago well enough to know what is being said. It's one part of the meeting the old people have to themselves. It pulls them together, separates them from the young, from the Chicago Indians, from the whites. They take their time; it's their right.

Now Mr. Billy Juan, the interpreter, says in Papago that the meeting should be blessed by Jose Vasquez since he has his good luck medal with him. This has not been mentioned in English so the people at the speakers table look surprised to see Jose rise and tip his hat.

Errol Flynn and Anna steady him as he walks to the center of the pool. He's doing a good job of keeping his eyes open today but he does have a little trouble walking down the incline. Now he holds on to Lone Wolf's chair.

"He looks real good," Mrs. Reyes whispers to Mrs. Domingo.

You can tell he's never blessed a meeting before. Still he knows what to do. His large stiff fingers finally get the leather thong around his neck untied and he holds up the little pouch before the group, lifting it as high as he can.

"Thank you, Jose Vasquez," Mrs. Domingo murmurs.

Other people nod approval.

Jose is wearing a new wide-brimmed Stetson hat.

Mrs. Reyes whispers to Mrs. Domingo, "Look at that good hat. You can sure tell he's got good luck."

"You can."

Jose sways slightly but, even so, this is an important day and he's doing an important thing. Everybody knows that's why he's willing to take the chance of taking the good luck medal out of its pouch.

"Special for this day," he says. "Okay, my friends, I'm going to let this here medal bless the whole meeting. Everybody."

He finally gets it out and holds it tightly between his thumb and forefinger. Everybody leans forward, moving closer to that good luck, but only little kids and old women actually go up to touch it. Mrs. Domingo and Mrs. Reyes are almost there when the medal slips from Jose's fingers and falls to the floor, rolls down the slope of the pool.

Jose bellows out. A dozen kids scramble. The Ramada Builder runs for it too and he comes up the winner, puts it in his mouth and covers his mouth with his hand.

"*Mine.* My good luck now."

Lopez and Manny and Gabriel run over to him. "Spit it out, man. That's not yours."

"*Mine.*" He has a hard time talking with the thing clenched in his teeth.

Jose is ready to fight for his good luck medal, but Manny sticks his hand in the Ramada Builder's mouth and gets it out.

Now of course the Ramada Builder is angry. He pushes his way toward the steps.

"Bunch of thieves!" he shouts back over his shoulder.

Before he climbs out of sight, Mrs. Domingo gets a tortilla and folds it and hands it to one of the children to take to him.

Manny wipes off the holy medal and hands it back to Jose but by now his hands are shaking wildly and he drops it again. This time Homer Lone Wolf leans down and grabs it before it has a chance to roll. He looks at it there in his hand and grins and shows it to Raymond Clear and shakes his head.

"Give it back or I knock your rotten head off," Jose mutters.

Errol Flynn and Anna tug at him.

Lone Wolf jumps up and pats him on the back. "Man, take it easy. You think I want a lousy subway token?"

People are very quiet. They're all looking closely into the Chicago Indian's face. Homer Lone Wolf laughs but the only person who joins his laughter is Raymond Clear.

Mrs. Domingo watches Jose's face as he puts his holy medal back into its pouch. You think that wino doesn't know what's going on around him, but sometimes he does.

Jose turns toward the people. "We going to listen to some guy who's so dumb he don't know a holy medal when he sees one! We going to sit here and listen to him?"

Mrs. Domingo wonders herself. He couldn't be too smart. But Gabriel comes to the Chicago Indian's defense.

"Listen, these guys didn't come here to talk about holy medals. They're here because they want to get Indians together all over the country. They want to talk Indian Power."

200

Jose Vasquez moves back across the room but he shakes his fist at Homer Lone Wolf as he goes. Homer Lone Wolf pretends not to notice. He stands up and smiles at everyone now as though nothing had happened.

"Indian brothers and sisters," he says, straightening his flowered tie. He spreads his arms like a preacher. "This has got to be the most important meeting you ever went to. I'll tell you why. Because it can change your life. That's why."

Lupe is groaning loudly now, holding her belly and swaying from side to side. The children pat her hands trying to calm her.

"I wonder if that lady shouldn't be in her own home right now instead of out at a meeting," Homer Lone Wolf suggests. "She seems a little bit upset."

"This *is* her home," Anna says quietly.

Mrs. Domingo says, "I think she likes the meeting okay."

So there is nothing for Homer Lone Wolf to do but raise his voice above Lupe's.

"He sure talks loud," Mrs. Reyes whispers to Mrs. Domingo.

It's true. Mrs. Domingo nods to her friend. They don't have to say anything else. Strange to hear Indians talk so loud. She doesn't think it's ever happened before in her life, never in all her childhood on the reservation. Chicago Indians must be different.

The Papagos sit very quiet, waiting for the words that are going to change their lives.

"All right," Homer Lone Wolf says, slapping his hands together. "The time has come to fight back. Listen, we Indians have been peaceful too long. I tell you, your brothers all over the country are demanding you stand up and fight. And tonight Mr. Clear and I are going to help you get started."

Mrs. Domingo wonders if they've brought guns with them. Are they going to sell them or just pass them around free at the end of the meeting? She exchanges looks with Mrs. Reyes, stubborn old lady looks that say those two silently agree not to put any guns against their shoulders. No matter what. Mrs. Domingo knows she's too old to start shooting people.

"They should put that man in the army," Mrs. Domingo whispers to her friend. "He sure is mad."

"I had a cousin like that," Mrs. Reyes answers. "From way out by Vaya Chin."

Homer Lone Wolf leans forward. He looks into the faces of his audience.

"We've talked to Indian groups all over the country and they're just like you – torn between two cultures, pulled apart emotionally. The society won't let you be one or the other. They keep you on the fence so you don't know whether you're Indian or white. Right?"

Mrs. Domingo and Mrs. Reyes look at each other in surprise. Mrs. Domingo knows that she herself feels no doubt. She's Indian. She's sure of that. The young ones nod. Right, man. That's right.

"Now let's start with just one simple example that's close to home. Okay? Look around you. Look at the *fine* place you've got to meet in. Look where Indians have to meet."

Mrs. Domingo isn't sure at first what he means yet she senses that he is making fun of her swimming pool, her gift from Jude. She knows the pool is beautiful, a bright blue, larger than any room she's ever lived in. If this man doesn't like it, let him take that up with St. Jude . . . .

"I ask you," he says, "do white people have to meet down in some abandoned swimming pool?"

Of course it's not abandoned. Eight people live down here. You call that abandoned? This man is crazy.

"A swimming pool without a drop of water in it! Not a damn drop."

Some meeting we'd be having down here if it *did* have water, she thinks. What does he want? To drown us all?

"It's a crime. All the white middle-class swimming pools are full of water in this town. Filled right up to the top with clear cool water. But the swimming pools of the Indian people are bone dry. Right?"

The young people agree with him. Right, they say. Right. "And it's a disgrace so we might as well begin right here. We might as well start by demanding water for this pool. Right?"

Right, the teenagers say.

Now Mrs. Domingo is worried. Holy Mother, give me strength. St. Jude, you're in this too. You better help me.

"This is just the beginning. There are a dozen important demands you've got to make but I tell you this . . . I promise you this. Before Raymond Clear and I leave this town there's going to be water in this pool."

The newspaper reporter is writing it down.

"Let me out first," Mrs. Reyes whispers. "I don't swim too good."

Now Mrs. Domingo stands up, raises her hand slowly.

"Listen, I think I'm going to say something because it's my swimming pool."

The Chicago Indian leans toward her. "Sure. You speak right up. Go right ahead. Tell us whatever's on your mind. That's what we're here for."

"Well, I just want to say I don't think water would be too good an idea. Because, see, it's a house we need so bad. And even if this place is shaped like a swimming pool, still it's not too bad a house now that we've got a good roof over it. I don't complain about this house."

She says it all very slowly and very quietly and her voice can only be heard a few rows away.

Now Raymond Clear is on his feet beside Homer Lone Wolf. He shakes his finger at her.

"Wait a minute, Lady. You've got to stop this thing of saying you're not going to complain. Damn right you're going to complain. Not just complain — demand!"

And Homer Lone Wolf says, "Think of the pleasure it would give this whole group, especially these poor disadvantaged children, if you had water in the swimming pool. Think of that before you start saying you don't dare ask for your rights."

She won't say anything else. She sits down, folds her hands in her lap, doesn't raise her eyes, doesn't want to see any faces now. She's embarrassed at having those loud voices directed toward her. The meeting goes on but she takes no part in it. Just thinks — I hope they'll give me time to get my stuff out, at least my shrine and my good chair before they start pouring water in.

CHAPTER 18

Maria Vasquez

Today a house can't hold her. She needs moving air. Wants wind, the kind of wind that presses through canyons out by Baboquivari Mountain. Indians know there's life in wind. That's one thing wrong with staying in a house too long; wind can't touch you there.

Not that she has a house to shut herself up in even if she wanted to. But if she did, say a real house with walls and windows and a door . . . even then she'd be outside today. She knows it. Half coyote, that's all she is. Why waste a house on her?

Everyone else is down in the swimming pool but she walks slowly past the entrance. Let them get other people's problems solved first. She'll just sit out here in the sunlight for a while. After all, she can be late. Her problems are so familiar now, they hang so easy on her, what's another hour with them.

This place has never been so quiet. Just the lonely long-tailed dogs pacing back and forth. Look how Elma Domingo's old shack seems ready to fall. It needs the noise of a dozen voices on all sides to hold it up.

Only the roofless ruins of the adobe house seem solid in the silence. Maria sits on that low crumbling wall. Sits heavily. She could be made of adobe herself. Good brown adobe inside her, not blood and bones and slime like white people. Dirt and maybe a few little stones and weeds.

See, even half a house can make you feel good if it is adobe. How many times in the desert has she seen ruins that still hold the spirit of thick sandy walls that stood amid the greasewood and the cholla a hundred years ago. But other houses — white people's houses — don't know how to stay alive when they are left alone. If you see machines tearing those houses down, you know they're already dead so it doesn't matter what is done to them. And of course those poor old tarpaper shacks like Elma Domingo's, they die even while people are still living there. What do you expect of something not made of earth or rocks?

Quiet as a weed, Maria sits watching her own hands. All week her hands have gone to her belly. They rest there now. She's not surprised any more. Just watches. Shakes her head. The body knows everything before the mind does anyway. You feel such knowledge inside yourself, such wordless knowing.

Though it's too soon to have proof, she knows she's pregnant. Doesn't think of this baby as Manny's any more than she thinks of the others as Jose's. They are hers. Not any man's. Only hers. They belong to her body, not her mind.

Hello, child. Remember, I promise you nothing. Don't count on me. But hello anyway, brown fat face. Crazy little wild thing. Lizard child. Coyote child. Prairie dog child. What's the difference except that animal creatures have an easier time making it through the world than human creatures. Old people on the reservation say animals walked the earth first so they've had time to learn the secrets people still haven't found out. They've had longer to learn how to get along in the desert. . . .

She looks up and sees Homer Lone Wolf climbing out of the pool, hurrying to the outhouse. When he comes back out, slamming the flimsy slat door, he sees her and stops.

"What are you doing here? Everybody's at the meeting."

"I'm on my way," she says, getting up.

He waits for her. "Come on. I need you down there. You gotta help me get some life into this thing."

She doesn't answer.

"Don't look surprised. I know all about you. Don't you remember we talked that night in the rain. You're the one who lives outside someplace . . . ."

"Over there."

"And I admire you for it." He puts his arm around her shoulder, pulls her along.

She doesn't know what he's thinking about. It's like listening to some white man talk. Crazy!

As they start down into the pool they hear shouts and screams and several children run past them up the steps. "Oh, my God, they're fighting," Lone Wolf says. "Breaking up the damn meeting!"

But it isn't that. Lupe is giving birth. That's all. Maria can't see her at first because Lupe is squatting down on the floor back against the wall where the battle is painted. The women are grouped around her, fifteen or twenty of them bending over her, encouraging her, murmuring. Old Mrs. Fuentes is holding Jose's good luck medal high above her and sometimes she brings it down like a swooping bird to light on Lupe's belly, her lips. People hurry up and down the steps for rags and water and herb broth and whiskey and rosaries.

Everybody knows about the witchcraft that has taken Lupe's mind and body too. Even the children know that anything can happen and they go up into the sunlight without being told. At times like this you depend on the old people, the wise wrinkled ones who still have some of the power of tribal teachings. They are the only ones who can call up mystical strengths to work against evil forces. You know they need quiet to shape their thoughts so nobody speaks at all.

Maria lets her hands go again to her own belly as she stands back listening to Lupe scream for help. The midwife has been called but there are a dozen women here who can do her job.

Suddenly Lupe is quiet and there is a gentle murmur spreading from the women surrounding Lupe to the people at the other end of the pool. A slow wave. Joyous. Everything is all right. It's a baby Lupe has thrust from her body, not a witch object after all. Thank God, a baby. A girl baby.

That *bruja* may have tried to make it something else but her power wasn't that great. For once some good luck, everybody says. They give Jose back his medal and clap Ignacio on the back and shake his hand. Surely things will be better now. This could be the beginning of a long period of good luck. That's the way it works, they say.

Even as Ignacio and Lopez carry Lupe and the new baby up the steps to put them to bed in the shack, people begin taking up a collection to buy wine. To celebrate the birth of a new child, wine for all!

"Wait a minute here," Raymond Clear calls out, waving his arms and climbing up on a chair to try to get people's attention. "Friends, I understand your desire to celebrate this fine occasion but we don't want to throw away our money on liquor. We're going to need cash to set up this Indian organization we came to talk to you about. Right? So everybody just put that money back in your pocket and . . . ."

A few people look up surprised to see him standing on a chair shouting. Nobody listens, of course. They are too busy collecting the wine money—$7.96.

"How about it," Raymond Clear yells. "Let's get back to our meeting. Let's accomplish what we came here for."

People take their places politely. Everything is quiet. Still, you can tell that Raymond Clear and Homer Lone Wolf and the young people around them are disappointed with the way things are going.

Homer Lone Wolf tries to grin about it as he taps the table with his pen. "As we were saying . . . about an hour ago . . . ."

The old people settle back. And the young people take turn's speaking of their hardships, their frustration, their poverty. Even Sue Mills speaks excitedly, emotionally, of Indian needs. Only the old people are silent. Not a word out of them when Raymond Lone Wolf calls for speakers.

Maria admires those young people, envies the way they pour out their feelings. She can't do that. Maybe her own kids will be able to. Talk out like a white man. If that's what you have to do to get your problems solved she may as well go back outside.

But of course she doesn't leave. She's sitting on a blanket on the slanting floor, leaning forward for balance. One of Rose's children comes over and dumps Carmen down beside her, damp and limp. Maria lifts her onto her lap and Carmen closes her eyes. Maria rocks back and forth as she sits there. She's rocking Carmen and the new no-name baby and maybe all the babies that have been in her body, maybe all the babies in the world. Rocking herself too . . . .

She sees Manny across the room but he might as well be a thousand miles away. He is with the men now. Look at his face. You can tell he's interested in the speeches. He's nodding with the Chicago Indians, *right . . . right.* He's as bold as they are. She looks at him with love. Admires his face. Wishes she could see his round belly.

Manny, like other men she's known, separates his life into many parts. She realizes that the part she shares with him on the mattress at night is far removed from his days of chopping cotton, from his detective course, from his beer drinking, his guitar playing. For her there aren't any separate parts of life, just one long breath. One breath that takes in every glass of beer, every yelling kid, every night of moving against a man in bed, every fear, every anger, every candle she's ever lit. One day is a part of the next one.

"Maria Vasquez . . . right over there."

She hears her name. Looks around quickly. Lifts her hands to her face.

Homer Lone Wolf is leaning toward her, speaking to her.

"Another example of what I'm talking about," he says. "A good example. And I hope she won't mind if I mention her because I think we have to be aware that some of our Indian people are just flatly rejecting the white man's way. . . ."

Maria looks down at Carmen asleep in her lap.

"Come on up here," Lone Wolf says.

Without looking at him, she shakes her head no.

"Well, okay," he says, "but I'm going to use this example anyway because it's something right in your own community. It's something everybody can understand."

Maria knows the people around her are as confused as she is. Who can even guess what's on this man's mind?

"Does this woman accept the white man's dictates as to how she is to live? No! She makes her own choice to raise her children in the traditional Papago way. This woman . . . this true Indian woman refuses a house. She refuses the four walls concept. She insists on living outside, close to nature the way her ancestors did. Right? Am I right?"

"Right," a few of the young people say.

The newspaper man is taking notes. He leans over and asks, "What's that name?"

"Maria Vasquez," Sue Mills tells him.

Lone Wolf continues. Won't let it end. No matter how hard Maria prays. On. On. On. . . .

"You have to have real courage to choose your life style this way. And personally I want to congratulate Mrs. Vasquez for saying NO to the white man. Okay . . . she goes right ahead and sleeps outside. Nobody's going to change her. And she's raising those five children to be proud and free."

Gabriel reaches over to try to stop him, maybe to let him know he's on the wrong track, but it doesn't do any good. The words go on.

Sue Mills jumps up and runs over to Maria and embraces her. "Don't be so shy about it," she says. "Be proud."

Still Maria can't look up. She doesn't want to see the way Anna's eyes blink in amazement or the way Errol Flynn is laughing, covering his mouth with his hands. Or Manny nodding slowly in appreciation of the wonderful traps and mazes that wait at the end of a thought.

Every Indian in the place knows Maria wants a house as much as anybody. They know she's tried all summer to find one. Who doesn't remember her walking down the alleys looking for something cheap enough? Any old shack.

Now that the people understand the error, they accept it as a good joke on the two Chicago Indians. In fact, a joke on Chicago Indians seems almost as good as a joke on white people. The old ladies in the back row smile. You can tell they are beginning to enjoy this meeting after all. They are too polite to laugh out loud but there is a little change in their breathing when Mr. Juan translates Homer Lone Wolf's speeches.

"I wish you'd come up here and tell everyone your experiences in this thing. How you personally managed to keep from giving in to the tremendous pressure you must have felt from the whole white community . . . ."

Maria shakes her head. Comfort me, she prays to Jude. Forgive me for putting my trust somewhere besides you. Imagine thinking I was coming down here to get my problems solved! Jude may not always help you but he sure doesn't very often humiliate you either so you're not risking anything. St. Jude, good friend, just keep me from hearing anything right now. Just that. And next week, a candle for sure.

Jude may be trying to help but it's still hard to keep from hearing that loud voice. Loud as a white man.

"Now suppose this brave determined woman had a strong Indian organization back of her. Suppose she had people all over the country to bring pressure and demand her rights! Do you begin to see the possibilities, friends? Do you understand what we're talking about?"

"I do," Sue Mills calls out. "It would be wonderful."

The young people nod. The old people look straight ahead. "But it can't be done without money," Raymond Clear reminds them. "U.S. money. Not wampum. And every one of you ought to get out and work for that money. Really give!"

But while he is speaking there is an interruption. The wine arrives and everyone welcomes the men who come bringing it carefully down the steps.

Good luck and a long and happy life to the infant. Good health and wisdom and many fine children. Saints' blessings on her. The blessings of her ancestors. The blessings of the Papago tribe and of their neighbors, the Pimas, those good honest desert people. Yes, and the blessings of this meeting.

Maria reaches for the bottle as it goes around. She herself does not offer a toast. Doesn't want to talk out loud. Even so, she nods to the new child in recognition after she has drunk her share of the wine. Maybe more than her share because she needs it. Maybe St. Jude sent that wine around to comfort her. Good friend Jude.

Finally she is at ease enough so that she can shake her head and smile when the people she knows come up and whisper and make jokes . . . small sympathetic quiet jokes.

"Yeah," they say, "you sure know how to keep from having to live in a house all right. You're sure good at that. You gonna move up to the caves? Up to the mountains? . . . Hey, Maria, I notice you don't mind being in a building so much if it happens to be a bar . . . crazy lady. . . ."

She wishes her friend, Rose, were here, not cooped up in jail. It would be good to have Rose sitting by her. Not that she'd say anything at all. But they've shared so many silences. They both know how to laugh or cry without showing a thing to anybody.

Papagos take such pleasure in a potluck supper. Maria feels the contentment around her, the sacredness of eating together as friends, and that too comforts her, warms her as the wine warmed her.

The women take their places with ladles and spoons to serve more and more pots of steaming frijoles. More tortillas are brought down the stairs. More chile. Voices are low and steady and easy but above the Papago sounds comes the voice of Raymond Clear.

"Now we're not quite through here, folks. I'm afraid those wine bottles broke up this meeting, but I'm sure you want to finish up the important part. Surely . . . ."

But the young people tell him he might as well wait. It looks like the old people have taken over serving the food and there isn't any way to stop people from eating now. Nobody is thinking about a meeting.

It's true. The swimming pool has become as Indian as a reservation feast house and it is filled with the same remembered good feelings, the same Papago voices. But Maria isn't at ease yet. A Papago doesn't like to be singled out for any reason, even for praise. Besides, that reporter keeps watching her. Is he waiting for her to finish eating? Maybe she should leave now. Just take Carmen and slip away.

But the reporter hurries over before she can make it to the steps.

"Listen," he says. "I think you're fantastic. Really great what you're doing. Now just a couple of questions . . . ."

Maria will try to get it over with as soon as possible. You say what you think white people want to hear, that's all. You remember that yes is always better than no.

"How many children?"

"Five," she says. Wonders if she should have counted Carmen. Hopes Mrs. Waterman won't find out.

"And I bet they love living out, don't they?"

"They never mentioned it," she says.

"And how long have you been living this way, just camping?"

She hesitates. They always want you to say things so exactly. "Since early summer maybe. I don't remember the month. A couple of other times too . . . now and then."

"All right. What prompted you to reject the white man's way of living? Something must have made you decide to stick to your own values . . . ."

She wishes to God he'd ask questions she could answer yes or no.

"I don't know, I just decided I guess. Anyway, I didn't have a house to live in."

"Do you feel that your rights are being violated in any way? Is the city pressuring you to move into a house?"

She tries to be truthful. Doesn't know anything about what the city wants. Never heard it mentioned.

"I guess the lady at welfare wants me to rent a house. She does. She wants bedrooms and everything. And a number."

"But you told her off?"

Maria shakes her head. *"Me?"*

"Of course," he says. "You wouldn't do it that way. I can tell that. You just go right ahead and follow your own beliefs no matter what anybody says. Right?"

Maria wishes her friends couldn't hear all this. "I got to leave. Really, I have work to do."

"Then I won't take but a minute more. Look, I need a picture of you wherever you're camped. Maybe you and a couple of the children."

A picture? She shakes her head no. Surely not. Does she have to do that? Here comes the man with the camera.

. . .

Homer Lone Wolf has been listening. "I'll go with you. You can be pointing out the place to me."

Maria looks around for Manny. Her eyes beg him. Come help me. You with your smart ways and your detective course brain. Come help me against this white man.

But the only one who comes is Amelia. "Mama, is it the law to have a house?"

Maria nods. "You come with me," she says.

Anybody is a help. Even Amelia. Nobody pushes her around. Right now, five years old, she's braver than Maria. Out in the sunlight Maria stands beside the mattress in the sandy yard.

"Look up. Look this way," the photographer says.

She can't. Looks down at the ground.

"Nobody tells her what to do," the reporter says. He's smiling at her.

"Okay," the photographer tells Maria. "You want to be talking to Mr. Lone Wolf? Maybe telling him how you won't live in a house. Go ahead and tell him."

Homer Lone Wolf stands beside her. It's no use. She still can't look up. Let them arrest her if they have to. She can't help it. Holy Mother! They even tell you which way to turn your eyes.

"Great. Fine. Now don't pay any attention to the camera. Just go ahead with whatever you're doing . . . ."

She stands stiffly, turned away from all of them, facing the mountains. The photographer squats on the ground, peers at the alley, the mattress, the buckets hanging from the mesquite tree, the iron pot of frijoles on the stove . . . her life looked at through the eye of that camera.

"You be sure to read the paper tomorrow," the reporter says to her.

She nods, still not looking directly at him.

"We better get some shots of that swimming pool too. But it's going to look pretty crazy with a junk heap like that on top of it."

"You guys do a good story and I bet you in a week that thing will have water in it," Lone Wolf says. "Less than a week!"

"Yeah, the Papagos better learn to swim."

Lone Wolf walks off with the reporter and the photographer and Amelia goes with them. Maria sits down on the mattress. Her hands go to her belly. Child, you sure picked you some mother. Some crazy mother who won't live in a house.

Suddenly she remembers Mrs. Waterman. That woman is going to be surprised tomorrow to pick up the paper and read about this Indian who doesn't want a house. Remembers how Mrs. Waterman was tricked into thinking she lived right over there in Elma Domingo's shack. Remembers how red her face turns when she's angry. Remembers the straight line of that mouth.

Well, at least she won't hear about it tonight. All Maria has to worry about this second is whether to spend a dime for a candle over at St. Jude's or to put another nickel with it and have a beer instead. She can't do both.

But she knows this: your feet decide such things for you. Just start walking and see where they take you. And if it's the B-29 they choose, don't worry. St. Jude understands his people.

219

CHAPTER 19

MRS. DOMINGO

There are always cars driving by now—white people's shiny white cars creeping down the alley and around the block. You see Anglos in sunglasses leaning out car windows looking at the shacks, pointing toward the swimming pool, taking pictures of the dark children who stand giggling at the fence.

It's the third day of the siege. Mrs. Domingo is huddled in the shack with Lupe and the baby and a few of the old people. She's glad she has friends to sit with her at a time like this.

"Surrounded," she says. "Captured. That's what we are."

"Be glad they're not Apaches," Mrs. Fuentes says. "That would be worse."

"I think I'd feel more at ease with Apaches."

Step out there and a television camera gets you. Somebody sticks a machine in your face and expects you to start talking. Well, Elma Domingo isn't crazy enough to start talking to machines. She doesn't talk much to people. Why should she talk to machines?

Every day you find a dozen Anglos ready to hit you with their questions. People you never saw before come running up and grab you and put their arms around you. Who knows what they're talking about? All you can do is laugh as politely as possible and back away.

Of course Mrs. Domingo pretends not to speak English.

That helps a little. At least it puts a fence around you but it's a pretty flimsy fence. It doesn't keep you from hearing those loud Anglo voices . . . .

Just look at that marvelous old face. Why don't you try to get a picture of her?

Look how primitively they live, poor things . . . .

Those long braids on that old one. Wonder if she's ever cut her hair.

Honestly, there's a lot of things they need more than a swimming pool, but I suppose if that's what they want so bad . . . .

It's probably a symbol to them. You know. It'll be the greatest thing that's ever happened to them.

Even so, you have to go out sometime.

Mrs. Domingo opens the door an inch and looks into the bright hot sunlight.

"Do I take me a white flag?"

The Indians smile. Her friend, Mrs. Fuentes, has been sitting beside her drinking black coffee.

Now Mrs. Fuentes gets up and stands beside her at the door. "Watch out," she says. "There's a lot of dust out there. Maybe more of them came when we didn't notice."

Mrs. Domingo take another quick look. "My God, they're tearing the roof off the top of the swimming pool. All that good stuff we had there. Just ruining that place. Now for sure we won't be able to use it for a house."

"Maybe you ought to try to talk them out of it," Mrs. Fuentes suggests. "You can talk pretty good."

Mrs. Domingo straightens her shoulders. "Well, it is my pool. I'm the one ought to say if it has a roof or water."

Sure, they agree. How come those Anglos can come along and make a mess of it? Them and those Chicago Indians.

"I'm on my way to put them straight," Mrs. Domingo says.

Still, she hesitates at the door. Well, why not? Anyone with any sense would hesitate to go out there.

She takes her walking stick, her good ironwood stick. Not that she needs it but it is a beautiful rich color, red-brown, finely polished and straighter than ironwood usually grows. That stick gives her confidence. It makes her look older, more important. When she points it an Indian will take notice. But who knows what makes an Anglo take notice?

Okay. Enough standing around. She steps out the door. The television camera is turned to the swimming pool and there must be fifty people watching those dressed-up white men tearing junk off the top of the pool. A few Indians too, back away from the camera. It's not too often an Indian gets to watch white men working, sweating in the sun. It's something to see.

Off comes the junk yard tin, the palm fronds, the old signs, the cardboard. Down comes the rickety little shelter that once kept rain out of the entrance to the pool.

Look at the Anglo men. They work so fast, faster than Indians. It doesn't take half an hour to remove what it took a full day to put together. Even those great long telephone poles across the width of the pool have to go. Two men at each end, both lifting at the same moment, hoist them easily and lay them aside.

It shouldn't be so easy to do something like that. It shouldn't take so little time. It shouldn't seem so unimportant.

She remembers what a joyous time that was when those poles were dragged in, the mystery and wonder of that small miracle when they saw that the length was right. Perfect. Perfect.

The Ramada Builder must have remembered too. Anyway, he starts to cry. He's standing back under the tree watching his work, his greatest ramada roof, being torn down. The finest thing he ever built . . . .

222

Mrs. Domingo goes over to him but she doesn't say anything. Just shakes her head, so he'll know she doesn't understand it any better than he does.

"Bastards," the Ramada Builder sobs, kicking at the dirt. "Look at them dirty white bastards."

He turns away. Can't stand to watch. Tears flow down his dusty cheeks. He sits in the dirt.

Mrs. Domingo looks around for Homer Lone Wolf or Raymond Clear. After all, she reminds herself, they are Indian, some kind of Indian, and they did come here to solve everybody's problems. Certainly they are the ones to handle this thing. It's not as though you had to talk to Anglos. Or maybe she can find Gabriel. So many strange faces here in her yard.

Finally she spots Lone Wolf. He's surrounded by white people, talking to them, laughing with them. Even so, she has to speak. She taps his arm.

"Well," he says, "you're just about the most famous little ole lady around. You know that?"

He hands her a newspaper but she doesn't look at it. "I came to say something about my swimming pool."

But he doesn't give her a chance. "Look here."

He opens the paper for her, puts it in front of her face.

DREAM COMES TRUE FOR LOCAL INDIANS
SWIMMING POOL FUND GROWS

"I don't have my glasses," she says. "Maybe I'll read it later."

He points to half a page of pictures. "What did I tell you?"

Even without glasses she can see them. There's Maria Vasquez and her kids over in the alley. There's the old tin shack too. And a picture of the neighborhood children, ten or so of them, just standing there beside the covered swimming pool. She admires that picture most.

"That's pretty. Real pretty."

"You want to save it? We got lots of copies."

"Maybe Jesus Gomez over there, him . . . the Ramada Builder . . . maybe he could have it. Maybe he wouldn't feel so bad if he could keep a picture of the way it used to look."

But Lone Wolf is reading the article to her. "Did you get that part about the fund?" he asks. "A lot of people are donating money to get the pool in shape. You won't believe it."

"Money?"

"You'll see, sweetheart. You'll be swimming in a week." He laughs and the people standing around him laugh too.

Mrs. Domingo turns away. But before she makes it back to her friends in the shack she sees a truck unloading something in the alley.

At first she can't tell what it is wrapped in so much cardboard. Just thinks how Indians could use good new thick cardboard like that. Then she sees something shiny, plastic, bright yellow with flowers. People untie paper and string. Everyone else seems to know. She thinks she's the last one to figure it out. Even the children are jumping up and down.

Finally there by the empty swimming pool, between the woodpile and the mesquite tree, they set a round redwood table shaded by a flowered beach umbrella. Then a chaise lounge with a matching flowered pad. Two chairs to pull up to that table.

Mrs. Domingo goes on toward the shack but one of the children runs to her with a message. "They want you to come sit on that new furniture for your picture. That's what the man said to tell you."

But Mrs. Domingo shakes her head.

"I got to go stir the beans," she says.

225

CHAPTER 20

Maria Vasquez

There's no other way. It has to happen. Mrs. Waterman will come. Her anger will shoot out. She'll have the book of rules in her hand and that book will show that Maria Vasquez must be punished for lying to a social worker, for pretending that she has a house to live in, for using somebody else's house number. Maybe for other things too. Who knows how many rules she has broken this week? Who knows what the punishment will be? Not jail, Maria hopes.

"We better go before she comes," Anna says. "We could be at somebody else's place for a while. Maybe over at Gonzales'."

It's true. An Indian will take you in. An Indian will share what little room he has and he won't ask how long you're going to stay camped on his floor or how much money you brought with you.

Out on the reservation they say that in the old days if one man killed a deer, everybody ate. When there was hunger in a village, the food was divided. Cactus fruit or mesquite beans or roots, it was all divided. Good luck was divided. How can good luck belong to one alone? To a Papago that makes sense. Forgive him for it.

Here in town it's hard for a Papago not to want to share with his brothers the way he did on the reservation. But here you have to be careful to keep the Anglos from knowing about it. You find out it's against the law to share your welfare food with a family down the street even though those people are just as hungry as you are. Yes, and you find out it's against the law to take in somebody else's children. Nobody knows why they have such rules. Things that make sense to an Indian are against the law in the Anglo's world. You just have to remember it.

Maria knows she could take the children and move in somewhere. That's true. Still, she won't do it. Something makes her wait for Mrs. Waterman to come.

"Mama, maybe she won't read about you in the paper. Maybe she won't find out."

"She'll find out."

"You think she'll be mad?"

Maria nods. "Sure, she'll be mad."

Even Manny is surprised that she doesn't want to gather up her cardboard boxes and go hide somewhere.

"They could say you're trying to defraud the government," he says.

"The U.S. government?"

"That or the county, either one."

"But remember, I didn't get no money. No money or no house either."

"That won't matter. That's the way they see it."

But for some reason of her own Maria knows she's going to wait for Agnes Waterman. She'll hear what that woman has to say. She'll find out the name of her crime and let things end as they will. Get it over with. Let it pass.

"What's in your head anyway?" Manny asks her.

She doesn't say. Doesn't know. People ask that like it's a simple question but it's not. It's the hardest question in the world.

"What are you thinking?"

Still she shakes her head. All she really knows is that she is alone. She's got nobody. Even with Manny in sight and the kids running back and forth and half the town over by the swimming pool watching the water pour into it at last, Maria is alone. Today she knows that. Her only companion is the child in her belly and she doesn't try to fool herself into thinking that's very much companionship. Even if she had a beer right now, that glass wouldn't be enough of a friend to help her.

Anglos who come to see the swimming pool always walk around looking for Maria's place too. They've seen the picture in the paper and read about her — Indian woman rejects housing — and they want to talk to her, but she doesn't know what to say to anybody. It's easier to go sit in the shack with Lupe and rock her new baby, Rosa, for her. It's good to move back and forth just humming, humming as she waits for Agnes Waterman.

That's where she is when Mrs. Waterman finally shows up.

There is a knock, the kind of knock Anglos make when they don't have all day to stand there in the hot sun at your door. When she hears the sound Maria stiffens. Still holding the baby, she opens the door.

"Well, Mrs. Vasquez! I didn't expect to find you sitting in a *house.*"

When Anglos say something like that they want an answer, but Indians don't mind just looking at them blankly as long as the Anglo wants to wait. After all, it wasn't a question. And it doesn't demand an answer.

"Is this where you live . . . or not?"

Maria shakes her head. She still hasn't really opened the door.

"One minute."

She hands the baby back to Lupe and goes outside and sees that, yes, Mrs. Waterman does have some kind of book in her arm. The book of rules.

Mrs. Waterman is standing in the shade of the chinaberry tree waving her purse at the dogs to keep them from sniffing her.

"Come over here, Mrs. Vasquez."

But Maria says, "No. We better go to the alley. To my place where I got my stuff."

She starts walking very slowly. Mrs. Waterman walks much faster, gets there first. She notices everything, even the beans in the pan on the wood stove.

"All right, Mrs. Vasquez. I'll say what I have to say fast. Children in this county live in houses. And if a mother doesn't even care enough about her children to house them properly then she doesn't deserve to have those children in her custody. Do you understand that?"

"Yes," Maria answers.

"Well, you ought to because we've been over it before. You don't seem to care though."

"I care."

"Well, this time we have to take the children away from you. The four of them. They'll go to foster homes. But if the time ever comes when you get yourself straightened out, then . . . ."

"What?"

She's surprised. She'd only expected them to punish her, not the kids too.

"Mrs. Vasquez, those children are what we call *neglected.* They don't have a roof over their heads because their mother doesn't choose to give them one. At least in a foster home they'll have a roof."

"I won't let them go." Maria stands with the sun in her face, her legs wide, her hands on her hips.

"Well, it's best for them. Now, look. You have to sign these papers. I'll just explain them to you so . . . ."

"No," Maria says. "I won't sign for you to take away my kids."

"Then we'll take them with a court order. You've had every chance in the world, Mrs. Vasquez. I've put up with a lot from you. And now this newspaper thing to get yourself a little publicity. Not wanting a house!"

"Well, that's my own business," Maria says. "Not yours."

They both look up, surprised. Maybe Maria is even more surprised than Mrs. Waterman. This isn't the way Maria talks to white women.

Her voice is as low and quiet and steady as ever, but words like that must be somebody else's words.

"And my kids are my business too."

Mrs. Waterman raises her own voice in reply. Her words come fast. No Indian could talk that fast.

"Well, I'm not making up my own rules. I'm telling you the law."

"And I don't care who made that law. I don't listen to that crazy law. You think I'd give my kids away?"

Maria Vasquez. She's dizzy with those words. She raises her head. For the first time in her life she looks directly at this woman. She faces her. Holy Mother. She's one of those Papago warriors in Gabriel's painting. Feels like she's got eagles flying over her, blessing her, giving her power. Can't tell whether she's shaking or not. Maybe she *is* crazy.

"Now you listen to me, Mrs. Vasquez. I'll be here at ten tomorrow and I expect you to have those children ready. Right here and ready to go."

"But they're not going," Maria tells her.

Mrs. Waterman's face is red. "We'll see about that!"

Maria feels the breath coming up into her lungs, feels desert winds moving into her body. Everything is unexpected. Magical. There is a force in her, a strength.

"Get out of my alley," Maria shouts. Bellows. "Just get the hell away from here."

She's wildly alive. She feels fine. Fine!

"Go on. I said get out."

Mrs. Waterman's face is fuzzy with disbelief. "I'm trying to *help!*"

Maria swings around, grabs a thin thorny branch right off the mesquite tree where the can of water is hanging. Raises that branch high in the air. *Warrior woman.*

Mrs. Waterman backs away. She looks quickly toward her car waiting at the curb. One hand reaching toward that car, she calls out, "I'm getting the police right now. You'll see. You just wait."

Maria can't stop swinging that stick. It's still in her hand when the car drives away and Indians begin to come over where Maria is. She finally turns around and faces the mountains. That's all she wants to see. Mountains. Strong hard bony desert mountains.

Somebody has told Manny and he comes running down the alley. Errol Flynn too. Anna. Amelia. Mrs. Domingo. Lopez. They know what's happened but even so they don't believe it.

"Mama. You! You were yelling at a white lady."

"Me."

Maria throws her stick down under the tree, starts gathering up clothes.

"What are you doing?" Manny wants to know.

"We got to head for the reservation before the cops come."

Manny tries to put his arm around her, but she doesn't need comfort.

"You can hide out someplace in town."

"Sure we can, Mama."

"No. We're heading out there. That's where I got to go. I'll get me a house there."

"How'll we get it?" Anna asks. "Will they give it to us?"

"Maybe we'll build it."

"I'm not going," Manny says. "I got enough to do in town. I can't go out there now. Anyway, you don't have to go either. You know that."

"In a way I have to."

Maria feels that loneliness again, lying like another child inside her. It's okay. She makes a place for it.

A box will be too hard to carry. She begins putting things in paper bags. One for each child. Not much. A few clothes. One pan. Cold tortillas for supper.

"I wonder is there somebody who'd give us a ride just to the edge of town where we can hitch. Somebody around here must have a car . . . ."

Mrs. Domingo nods. "There's a kid over there with a car. Gabriel's friend. That red car. I think it's running."

She goes to ask him. Anna and Amelia run to find Carmen and Jane. And Maria pours water in a glass jar, puts that jar in one of the paper sacks. Stands looking at her possessions scattered on the ground.

"Maybe you could sell that old wood stove for me," she says to Manny. "We'll come in and get the money sometime. We'll look around for you . . . ."

He reaches in his pocket and hands her two dollars.

"You take this now though. I don't know what you're going to do. Man, you're going crazy taking off like this."

Manny who knows everything . . . knows nothing now.

She can't touch him or it would be too hard to leave. Just looks at him and looks away. Even though he's still here for another minute or two, she knows it's over. She's alone. There isn't much time. Everybody knows it won't take the police car long to arrive. You can count on ten minutes, twenty at best. If the kid with the car doesn't come soon, they'll have to start walking.

But he comes. "You want a ride?"

"Out south," Maria tells him. "Just there by the highway. Somebody will stop for us there."

"Get in."

It's not often they are in a car. They don't really know anyone who has one. And Carmen has never been in a car at all, not one that runs. Only the abandoned one they play in.

Mrs. Domingo stops them. "Maybe Carmen ought to stay here awhile. I'd keep her. Or any of them, any of the little ones. Maybe the big ones can help you build a house but the baby'd just be in the way. Okay?"

Maria shakes her head. "Seems like I want them all for company right now."

So they go. All of them sitting close together, not saying a word. A lot of Indians are standing there watching as they drive away. Manny too. Maria keeps her eyes on him until they turn the corner but she doesn't wave or call. There isn't anything to say.

Two blocks away Maria asks the driver, "What if I stopped for just one second over there by Jude?"

He shrugs. He wouldn't go there himself but he slams on the brakes when he gets to the shrine.

"Be careful if you don't want the cops to see you. They come right down this street."

"It's for one minute only."

There's nothing to say to Jude either really. Still you feel like he's your best friend in town and you don't leave without at least a nod. It would be good to give him something to remember you by but when all you've got in the world is stuffed into a few little paper sacks, he'll forgive you. Well, Jude, old friend. . . .

"Come on," the boy behind the wheel calls out.

"Here I am."

So they're on the way. A glance at the B-29 bar as they go by. The cathedral. The secondhand store. People she knows, slow, tired Indians at the bus stop. Nobody sees Maria Vasquez passing by in that red car. Nobody waves goodby.

It's not far to the highway that takes you through the reservation. They say that highway keeps on going west until it reaches the ocean. Maybe it's true.

Now the car stops. Here's where they get out, each one except Carmen carrying a paper bag. They watch the red car turn back to town, watch it out of sight. Then they move to the side of the road, back in the dirt, facing the direction they want to go, west, toward the lowering sun. They are close to mountains now, jagged rough little mountains, piles of cactus and rocks.

Maria is impatient. After a lifetime of quiet waiting, she's surprised at herself. *Come on somebody. Pick us up. Take this crazy Indian home. We got to get there before night.*

It's a while. An hour maybe. Then a green pickup truck stops and they climb in back. Maria ties her scarf over her head. They turn their faces to the wind and ride in silence. It seems so fast, so beautiful to be rocked in the back of that truck, wrapped up in wind, dust stinging them roughly.

Maria sings as they drive along. You can't really hear her over the noise of the truck and the wind but the children look at each other. They've seen her drunk but they've never seen her like this. They don't know her. She doesn't care. Opens her mouth and wails out. It isn't sad. Not angry either the way her voice was when she yelled at Agnes Waterman. She feels it's more like the way a coyote calls to the moon, or the way hawks cry when wind lifts them, or the way a mountain lion plays with his own voice.

So they're going home. She's glad it is in the back of a truck. Remembers the truck that brought her over this same road the first time she came to Tucson. *God, I should have jumped.*

At the edge of the reservation the truck stops. The man comes around and says, "Well, this is it. I've got to turn here."

Maria nods. Anyway, they're this far. They're on Papago land.

"How much farther you going?" He looks at them as they climb out.

"A way," Maria says, very low. Like a reservation woman she moves her head to point the direction.

The truck drives off and leaves them standing there by a greasewood bush, all of them looking around at the open desert. The youngest ones are quiet as a bunch of rabbits. They're field mice. They're her own desert creatures, brown as prairie dogs, dry as lizards.

"Look over there," she tells them. "See, that's Baboquivari. That's the Papagos' sacred mountain where *I'itoi* lives."

They turn their faces toward that high rough cliff. Even Carmen looks that way.

"Papagos like to be where they can see that mountain. You're safe when you see it."

"Then we're okay," Amelia says. "Can't no cops get us."

They watch that mountain while they walk. Maria doesn't want to stand still any longer. She has to be moving. That's what her body tells her so that's what she does.

She knows that's how you stay alive . . . just doing what you must. Like any coyote back in the hills, like any skinny weed bending down so its roots won't be blown out of the sand, like any rattlesnake moving to the warmth of a rock in the sun.

And right now all she has to do is walk down the reservation road with her kids. All she has to do is keep singing like a fool.

CHAPTER 21

St. Jude

A lizard is already there when Mrs. Domingo stops by. She stands back, doesn't want to disturb this small desert brother. He's as out of place in town as the rest of Jude's people. He's as dusty and as quiet as the rest of them too.

She watches his breathing, his moving throat, the flick of his tongue, glimpses his turquoise blue underside as he lifts himself onto a rock. He's so close to the life force of the earth, low against the sand like that, it reflects in his eye. It moves him.

Now Mrs. Domingo has her turn before the saint. To tell the truth, she doesn't want to bother him with every little thing that goes wrong. Really, she hopes he doesn't know the swimming pool is full of water — he'd be so disappointed. No, she isn't here for that. She's come to light a candle for Maria Vasquez. Maria always liked the red ones best. A red one then for her today.

Jude's people don't stay put. They wander around a lot, but this saint understands that a city can't be home to desert people.

A Papago will just take off across the hills some afternoon and Jude won't see him again for years. Never mind what promises he's made for tomorrow morning. Man or woman, it's the same. Jude doesn't mind though. He knows his people are cousin to the land out there. Kin to rocks and weeds and maybe lizards too.

Jude doesn't forget them when they take off and they don't forget him either.

St. Jude, old friend, how about this? Let anyone who passes by speak for all the others who can't make it. We all need the same thing anyway. Just find a good safe place for lizards and for people too.

BYRD BAYLOR

Born in Texas, Byrd Baylor has always lived in the Southwest, mainly in Southern Arizona near the Mexican border. The Papago Indians, now called the Tohono O'odham Nation, are her neighbors and close friends.

Byrd writes from the heart about these peaceful, easygoing Native Americans, with respect born from her love of the people and their way of life. She injects a sense of humor into this story, which sustains the dignity of each culture.

Byrd is best known for her numerous award-winning children's books, such as *When Clay Sings* (a Caldecott award winner), *I'm In Charge Of Celebrations, Amigo, The Way to Start A Day*, and many more.

LEONARD F. CHANA

Leonard F. Chana was born in the fall of 1950 into the community of Kaij Mek (Burnt Seed), now called Santa Rosa Village, in the heart of the Tohono O'odham Nation.

Self-directed, Leonard began to follow his artistic gift in the early 1970's. He developed his own personal style of stippling (pen and ink) for expressing O'odham life and traditions. (There is no strong tradition of Tohono O'odham drawing.) Acrylic Paintings are a fairly new stage of his development.

Leonard resides in Tucson, where he works on his art creations, emerging from deep within his cultural heritage.